LABYRINTHS OF LIGHT

Book 3 The Stoneman Series

Terence Munsey

Munsey Music

Toronto Los Angeles London

LABYRINTHS OF LIGHT

published by:

Munsey Music

Box 511, Richmond Hill, Ontario, Canada, L4C 4Y8

Fax: 905 737 0208

© 1995 by Terence Munsey

Canadian Cataloguing in Publication Data

Munsey, Terence, 1953-

Labyrinths of light

(The stoneman series ; bk. 3)

ISBN 0-9697066-2-6

I. Title. II. Series: Munsey, Terence, 1953-
The stoneman series ; bk. 3

PS8576.U57L3 1995   C813'.54   C94-932211-3
PR9199.3.M86L3 1995

Library of Congress Catalogue Number 95-94007

First Munsey Music original soft cover printing   1995

Cover art design & back note © 1995 by Terence Munsey

Manufactured in Canada

Acknowledgments

Thank you to Christina Beaumont for the many hours of proof reading and for her editorial suggestions. It is greatly appreciated.

Thank you to Stewart and Evelyn for helping to answer some of my many questions.

Thank you to Jack Corman for the laser printer.

Thank you for the help of 'Ydnew'.

This book is dedicated to Fred.

Books by Terence Munsey in
The Stoneman Series:

THE FLIGHT OF THE STONEMAN'S SON

ISBN 0-9697066-0-X

LCCN 93-93660

Book 1

THE KEEPER OF THREE

ISBN 0-9697066-1-8

LCCN 93-86550

Book 2

LABYRINTHS OF LIGHT

ISBN 0-9697066-2-6

LCCN 95-94007

Book 3

MARKS OF STONE

ISBN 0-9697066-3-4

Book 4

Available at your bookstore

Author's Note

The Stoneman Series has been for me a wonderful happening. I started writing it in the summer of
1991, in Richmond Hill, overlooking my back garden with its flowers and trees. At the time, I was
looking for something magical to read, but not the
standard fiction or fantasy that was on the shelves.
I wanted a magical adventure that would be fun
and exciting, while at the same time having some
depth and mysticism.

Not being able to find any such new books by
others, I decided to write one. Having never written a novel before, I initially intended to write a
page or so a day until I eventually had a completed
novel, but quickly found myself engrossed in
writing the first book. After spending about eight
weeks of eighteen hour days of writing, I soon
realized that this was to be more than just one book
of the awakening and journey of: Julian, Darla,
Thiunn and Eruinn.

The first book wrote itself quickly and with great
pleasure on my part. It became for me a movie in
my mind and I merely transferred it from visual
thought to print. After it was finished, the 'movie'

continued to play in my mind. I began to see the next episode.

When I sat down to start the second book in the following summer, it quickly fell to the page. This time however, the story began to take on more life. The settings were stronger and the characters more focused. They had become very intimate friends and places. I still find myself re-reading parts of the prose from time to time in order to be reunited with these beautiful people and the Worlds in which they live. It brings a sense of calm, peace, and joy. By now, I had a very strong impression of the series and again looked forward to the following books /episodes.

It was at this point that <u>The Flight of the Stoneman's Son</u> was published. I found myself the author of a fabulous new adventure fantasy series, going from bookstore to bookstore promoting and book signing. I began to meet people who were excited to read 'Flight', and soon heard of their enjoyment after their reading, by their written correspondence or by meeting them at book signings. It was encouraging to discover a beginning readership to the series. Many of these readers were enjoying the story as well as the other subtleties of awakenings within the characters, and began pointing out other possible greater meanings. I was, and am fascinated by the response.

In January of 1994 I finished the third book Labyrinths of Light, in Pompano Beach, Florida, and upon my return home soon continued the 'movie' into book four: Marks of Stone in Richmond Hill, and in Picton, Ontario amidst the trees and sand dunes of Westlake.

'Labyrinths' is the bridging book between two and four. It is intended to add more depth and a notion of 'time' to the series. It is the book that both continues the adventure, while adding new dimensions in style and thought to the series.

With the release of book two: The Keeper of Three in August 1994, the series was securely launched. The readership had grown and the series was being accepted and read by not only fantasy / sci fi, but also general fiction fans. People are enjoying the story as I still do.

I know you will love this third book in the series: Labyrinths of Light, and I thank you for helping to make The Stoneman Series a success by buying, reading and telling people about it. Book four: Marks of Stone, will be out in August 1996.

Enjoy the worlds of Jard.

Terence Munsey.

Just when you begin to realize who and where
you are, you know how you aren't.

I'm sure, I'll be just fine. Thank you for the...the help. I'll just settle in and have some tea. Are you certain you won't share a pot with me?" Lenore was emotional. Being back in her little cottage in Jard was what she wanted, but there was also a new silence to her home. A silence that she had not anticipated. It was as if the cottage itself was sad or in mourning for the missing young ones.

"No thank you, we should get back and tidy up. If we see or hear anything from Julian's, we will let you know right away. Are you sure you wouldn't be more happy with us, there's plenty of..." room. Mrs. Reed was about to say, but was cut short by Lenore, who was eager to be alone. Not that the hospitality and comfort of the Reed's had been unwelcome. She just didn't want to be pampered or have to respond to their unspoken sympathy any longer. She needed to be alone. To try and cope on her own; to deal with whatever the outcome was to be. Something within her was calling. She was not able to understand the source, whether maternal instinct or something else—she was puzzled at what else it might be. She wanted to be alone now. She wanted to be free from all the worry, but she knew that was not possible.

"I'll be alright. You don't have to worry. I've missed my little cottage. It's time I got back into the routine of normal living. Now that all the fuss is over..."

It was obvious by the look in Lenore's eyes that she was trying to be strong, but tears were close behind them. Andof prevented their swelling forth by empathetically interjecting:

"There, they'll be back soon. Just think of the stories you will all have to tell!" It was a cheery thought, one that gave hope and briefly uplifted everyone's spirits.

"Yes, you're right. Well, I'd better get on my

way, and start cleaning up the place. Thank you again..." The Reeds began to make their way out.

"I'll come round to visit tomorrow." Mrs. Reed quickly added as she and Andof exited.

"That would be fine. Till tomorrow then..." Lenore stood stoically by the entry. "Good-bye."

"Good-bye."

Mr. and Mrs. Reed reluctantly turned and headed down the pathway back the way they had come, to return to their own home. They were concerned over leaving Lenore alone in her little cottage. During all the panic and evacuation caused by the recent events, the two of them had grown much closer to Lenore. She had become like a daughter to them. The Reeds had no young ones of their own. They were considerably older and patronizing in their ways. They had always kept to themselves, yet also kept a watchful eye on the comings and goings in their community. Lenore had always thought on Mrs. Reed as nothing more than a small minded provincial gossip. She had never developed a friendship with them beyond the formal politeness between 'not of choice' neighbors. Now this was to be changed. The Reeds had been strongly there to support and adopt Lenore during her need. They had shown another side, a side that Lenore had never known existed. She now began to feel a slight affection, as one would give to parents. She was not alone in the Worlds any longer. Though she longed for her own family, she felt a little less panicked and isolated. For that feeling, Lenore was grateful to the Reeds. She was grateful to them for taking her with them during the evacuation. She had had nowhere else to go and no-one else to which she could turn.

They had all gone farther south to Andof's brother's home in Pers, for safety from the possibility of invading Gotts. It had not taken long to get there. They traveled very lightly without encumbrances. A change of clothes and one or two personal items were all that any of them carried. There were many on the pathways south, but there was not a sense of panic amongst those evacuating their homes. Jardians were so disciplined in all that they did. A positive attitude was presented, whether it was false or not, did not matter. There was humor and high spirits. This had helped Lenore as she had gone along with the Reeds, leaving everything behind. Lenore recalled wondering if they would all be the same again. They, in her case meant: Julian and her two young ones, and the family that it made. The effort by all those around them on the journey away from danger had helped to raise her hopes of returning her own personal world, as well as Jard, back to normal.

After half a sun rise they arrived in Pers and were greeted affectionately by the Reed's family. Lenore was quickly made to feel that she belonged and was a part of their extended family. It was comforting during all the commotion of the recent events. It was a 'calm before the storm' feeling. No one knew how long they would have to remain as refugees, but they felt safe and at 'home'. Lenore hoped that all the other evacuees were feeling as secure in their own situations.

The Reeds were a large clan. There was one other brother, two sisters with their families, and a multitude of nephews and nieces. The home they were in was originally the homestead of Andof's parents. It was a large sturdy home made of the finest stone, and a beautifully thatched roof. It was three stories and large enough to be an Inn. It was here that, except for Andof, the family had remained, even after the passing of Andof's parents. Lenore learnt that

Andof and his wife had decided to move to Jard shortly after his parent's passing, Andof's younger brother had remained. It was the custom of those of Pers. Though not many in this age still followed the old ways, there were enough that still did. The older moved on and the younger remained. This allowed growth within the family by allowing the oldest and wisest to find newer opportunities that might benefit the rest of those left behind. The youngest would be charged with sustaining and caring for the rest that remained. This included not only parents, but also any other siblings that there might be. The move had been sad, but it was not a begrudged one. It was seen as a birth from a death. The natural order from which came balance. It was their way.

With all these new insights into the intimacies of the Reed family, Lenore soon relaxed and felt less emotion of her own pain and losses. It was a nice feeling. She prepared herself to become comfortable here in Pers, but within two sunrises the threat had passed and their emergency was over. The invasion from the North had been concluded as fast as it had begun. Andof and his wife had offered to remain here with Lenore, and not to return to Jard, but Lenore upon the news of the conclusion to the Gott invasion, became eager to get home. 'Perhaps her family would be there!' The Reeds did not argue, they understood. They left as quickly as they had arrived on the next sunrise.

All the way back from Pers Lenore had been of the highest hopes and spirit. She sensed something. She knew her family was alive. Her pace was strong and determined. She couldn't wait to get home to see if 'they' had returned. Now Lenore was back at her home, but 'they' were not there. She felt let down but still sensed her family was near, especially Julian. She could not explain the feeling.

Lenore waved as the Reeds walked down the pathway. She was pleased to be home, but troubled with her misreading of her intuition on her family. The feeling had been deep and strong. She had felt a connection, especially with Julian. She had believed this to mean that they were here in Jard, or at least very close by. She was confused when they were not here. The feelings were so strong.

All of her life Lenore had sometimes had feelings or intuitions about people and events. She had learnt to respect these intuitions or premonitions as they had always come true. This time they had been so strong that she was unsettled at misreading her sensing. She knew she had had the same type of 'feelings' on many other occasions, but this one had not ended the same as those others. The confusion was leading to a troubled feeling. What was wrong? All of these emotions ran through her as she watched the Reeds disappear from the path towards their cottage. When they were out of sight, she closed the door and retired to her sitting room that overlooked the side garden and the forest wilderness beyond her property. Perhaps she needed to rest. So much had happened, perhaps her feelings were being muddled by all the extreme changes over the past few sunrises.

Lenore spent the rest of that first sunrise calmly at home. She tried to empty her mind of her unsettled feelings, and expectation of her family returning. She busied herself by cleaning the cottage and reestablishing her usual cottage routine, but the feelings within her grew. They would not co-operate with Lenore's will. They slowly began to become more focused and intensify. They were centering on her brother. Something was wrong, but Lenore did not understand.

These new premonitions were very much

stronger than her normal feelings. Lenore was noticing a gradual loss of her own identity within herself, her ability to control or channel her intuitions, and the rising up of something or someone else. It frightened her. This newer personality was not malevolent. It was a part of her, but at the same instant it was more than her. It was of greater depth and age. It had a sense of many but also just one. Lenore tried to busy herself even more to distract her awareness of this unsettledness within her person.

By mid eve, there was nothing left to clean, and though she was fatigued she could not shut out the awareness or feelings within. This was disturbing to her. She knew that she must sleep or she would be in worse condition. Against her normal practice she resolved that this eve she would take some of the medicine that the doctor had left for her after the disappearance of Julian, Eruinn, and Thiunn, if she could not find sleep normally. She wanted to sleep. She believed that if she had to take it, the medicine would stop the feelings and help her to fall to a restful sleep.

At the normal time that Lenore would go to her bed, she did again this eve. She methodically went through her personal ritual of preparation for sleep: putting on her cozy nightgown, warming some milk and black syrup, reading a few pages of the days news, and then turning out the bedside lamp, pull the fluffy warm covers up over her, and fall into sleep.

She closed her eyes and lay waiting in her bed. She was unable to calm her mind enough of her worries, to sleep. She now knew she would remain restless, listless and awake. Even in Pers she had not rested well. She had not been able to sleep for any length of time since the vanishing of her family; only in fits and starts, just enough to allow her to raggedly survive. She had hoped that by returning to her home, she would finally find some solace and be able to better cope. Instead, it had only reminded her more of their absence. Every item within her cottage brought back the memories of her family and their loss. Her mind was in agony, especially tonight. She sat up and turned on the light, looked over to her bedside table, picked up her drink and determinedly took the medicine. Tonight she needed help to sleep, her insomnia had been going on too long. She put down the drink, turned down the light, and again settled herself snugly into her bed. She waited for the drug to work.

Quite some time passed and Lenore felt no change. Despair filled her as the stress swelled within her. Tears grew in her eyes. She began to weep. As she wept, she became distracted. She began to think that someone was in her room. This alarmed her. The image was trying to speak to her: *'Do not worry. All will be well soon.'* This echoed in her thoughts, though she did not see the lips moving of the person in her room; the voice was coming from that image. Then the image suddenly vanished in a blink of her eyes. This only added to her anguish.

She questioned whether she was going mad, now that she was having these hallucinations and was hearing voices. She wept more. The drug surreptitiously began to induce its effect. She was so upset, that without realizing, she was slowly succumbing to its soporific effect. She let herself go. She did not fight or question any longer. She had no choice. The drug was now in control. The drug was diminishing her thoughts. Though she was afraid of letting go of the control of her consciousness, she welcomed the peace, the silencing of her 'spirits'. With this in her mind she finally succumbed.

Once Lenore's conscious mind was completely under the control of the drug, her unconscious began to awaken. At first she dreamed of pleasantries. These were more images of feeling of well being; of the relaxation from the turmoil she had been constantly dealing with before the drug numbed her. She began to dream of her past; the careless abandon of her youth. Then suddenly this changed. She felt a fear that she had never felt before. There was a danger. She did not comprehend. Was it her? No, she abruptly understood. It was very old and from a past she had never lived in, but somehow she had. She began to toss and turn violently. She felt as if some shared part of her was about to be extinguished by an ancient darkness. She searched her feelings for some identity of the origin of the threat and the shared awareness that was being confronted. Everything was passing so quickly. She was one and many. She was herself and more. Her anguish climaxed:

"No. STOP!" Lenore screamed out as she slept. "No. You will not have him. He will not go." Her heightened clairvoyance understood and was acting faster than her cognizance.

"He will be mine. Do not interfere with me. You are no match. I will have him!" came the menacing voice in her dream. "We have worked too long to come to this point. His life is meaningless. Like you, we will devour all of those who are set to oppose us."

"You will not have him. I will not allow this to pass. Beware!" Lenore was confronting this *Evil* within her dream. The part was believable, though poorly acted, and her emotions were very involved with the dramatics of the scene. Her voice sounded poetic and proud, in the style of an actor reading clichéd lines. She heard its haunting quality.

In this dream, Lenore was standing tensed and ready to battle. In front of her there was an opaque cloud which contained a faint concealed image of something or someone very old. It was not clear to her. Other than the cloud and this partial image, there was no other scenery, just a dark void. She felt the danger of this cloud entity in *her* world. It did not belong there.

It was such a strange dream. Never before had she had such a nightmare. She had not expected this nightmare. Now she was imprisoned in her sleep, in this dream, by the drug and unable to awake from the it!

"Keep away!" she warned as the cloud and image became more clear as it approached her. "I have great Magic and will not hesitate to use it upon you."

Lenore didn't understand what she meant, but as she viewed the scene from her dream, she knew that this was true. Every fiber of her dreaming person felt the shiver of its malevolence. She was feeling extremely exposed, and threatened. Something was very foreign about its presence.

"Jur hzil mon nuun red ut yik low bu." she heard herself saying these old words. Though she didn't understand their meaning, she was very aware of their purpose. She was calling upon the Magic; the Magic that she as a daughter of the Stoneman's son, lay hidden in the greatest depths of her being.

"Nik, wroo bien ha! Nik, wroo bien ha! Nik, wroo bien ha!" Still the cloud and image approached.

"You think the mere uttering of those words will save you! Ha. How young you are! You are no match, now that I am so close to obtaining the secrets!" the translucent image spoke from its opaque shell with an *Evil* raspy tone. There was a hint of arrogant humor to it.

Lenore, startled by this utterance, stepped back. She instinctively raised her body into a rigid full upright stance. She looked vehemently at it, as she raised up her arms, crossing them in front of her face forming a cross that might shield her from this creature. Her hands were outstretched like claws of the great Bullar. Again she spoke the ancient words:

"**Ici Ni Ban yi**." she spoke boldly without fear. She was determined and confident. She held no anxiety for her own well being, but would protect her blood line passionately to the end. The *Evil* may win this battle, but it would not survive long thereafter. She would not permit it to harm her progeny!

There was a vile deep rasp of a retort from the *Evil*, and just as the time when it was against Thiunn in his Uncle's cottage in Jard, there came a sudden beam of energy from within the cloud. Lenore quickly lowered her head and shielded herself by the use of her arms. It was aimed at her. The energy beam was bent and sheared off to one side after striking Lenore's 'shield' of arms. Within moments another beam shot from the cloud. This time it met with Lenore's shielding arms and held. It did not bend off, but remained steady. Lenore was now in a struggle against this power. Somehow she was managing to hold her ground. She noted her confidence within the dream, but this could not last indefinitely. She must act quickly. *There was not much time*. She paused on that thought. It had a greater meaning that she couldn't comprehend.

The urgency of her present need hurried her beyond much more exploration of its duplicity in meaning. While she continued to push against the beam, she began to repeat what she had just said:

"**Ici Ni Ban yi. Ici Ni Ban yi. Ici Ni Ban yi.**" Each time she spoke the words, there was a noticeable weakening of the beam from the cloud. "**Ici Ni Ban yi. Ici Ni Ban yi. Ici Ni Ban yi.**"

The *Evil*, angered by this impertinence, began to intensify the strength of the beam. It was a tremendous clashing. The noise of the *Evil's* beam as it continued to hit Lenore's arms was deafening. There was a rippling of the energy all about her as the beams sheared off and fell all around. The display was staggering, but it could not overcome her magic.

"See how you are no match for my power!" The voice was directed at Lenore, who was visibly under a great strain and tiring. "I will put an end to you and all of your line!" There came again the laugh.

With the stating of his threat, Lenore dug deep within herself. She would not go down without doing some harm of her own. She began to twist her hips in a rocking motion. She made a circle. Slowly she moved as she held off the beam.

Then faster and faster, till suddenly, there came a brilliant flash of amber light from between her arms. This flash briefly neutralized the *Evil's* beam, causing a blinding light. When this burst had subdued Lenore was gone from sight. The *Evil* was stunned, as well as the sleeping Lenore.

1

“What an odd feeling.”

All of Julian’s senses were alive! There was such a tremendous amount of information about his present situation bombarding him. He was not able to focus too long on any of this sensorial input.

As Julian fell deeper into the abyss, he began to experience a strange sensation. He was going in and out of what he thought was a semi conscious state. He began to imagine he was partially somewhere other than in his falling into the abyss. It was almost a dreamlike experience. Part of him was in another very strange place. He did not understand what was causing it. He was finding himself being distracted from his present reality, and fears. He was aware of being in the abyss, and at the same time elsewhere. Gradually the 'elsewhere' was overpowering his consciousness.

As he continued to fall, he began to see more definition of this other awareness of place, this other reality. Somehow he knew he could go there. There was a brilliance exuding from it. In his half conscious mind, he tried to make visual sense of the lights and fast changes being thrust upon his awareness from this other place. He began to clearly identify that it was a shaft of some sort, in a dark void. He found his limited view within this shaft disorienting. It was hard for him to orient himself as he was drifting between awareness of his falling into the abyss and falling into this shaft. He felt as though he was being pulled more and more into this shaft, and farther from the abyss.

Out of an increasing curiosity, he began to focus his attention upon this shaft place. He found himself laboring to see more. His eyes were starving for more. More light, more of anything that was concrete and of depth. His eyes were becoming sore from the strain of the tunnel like vision from within this shaft. It was a shock to him, having been used to unlimited sight in every direction, and then forced into long narrow shafts surrounded by a black nothingness.

As his awareness fell more totally into the shaft, the only thing that made sense to him was that he could not expect this shaft or the black zone it was in, to represent anything 'normal' according to his conceptualization. There would be no relief from this strain upon his Jardian perception. His only remedy was to fix his glance down the shaft, concentrating with what narrow sight he had, looking for, or anticipating any fluctuations or sudden intrusions there might be from the blackness. His body was very tense and all his other senses heightened in this anticipation. He was now mostly aware of only his existence within this shaft.

"Where am I?"

He did not spend too much thought on this question, as, nearby to his left, another shaft of circular light which he assumed was similar to his, suddenly shot into his peripheral vision, and across in front of where he assumed his shaft was moving. It appeared that this shaft would collide with his. Julian tensed. His spine was tingling from the stress. His neck was sore, and the lower part of his back, where his spinal cord joined his hips was trembling. From the spasms of pain, it felt as if his lower back would take control of itself and Julian left the involuntary victim to its whim. In fact, if he was not somehow being totally supported and kept in place by the energy exuded within this shaft, he would not have been able to keep upright. He would have collapsed under the conditions. It was odd to him, but beyond his present discomfort. As he was maintained by this force in his place, there was a strange notion of serenity deep within him. This glint of composure gave him the strength to withstand the pain that began to radiate from his back up his spine and into his shoulders, as he awaited the inevitable collision. Then, just as suddenly as the other new shaft had appeared from the reaches of his peripheral sight, it turned and passed by without harm. Other than within his own sole remaining shaft, there was blackness once more in the void!

After several more moments of expectation of

other eruptions from the void of blackness, and seeing none, Julian began to relax. He now became acutely aware of the aches and pains of his stressed muscles. Looking down, he noted that his hands were almost white from the tight fists that he saw he must have made during the ordeal. He was surprised by this reaction, but accepted that under these circumstances his instinctual being was obviously more in control than his rational.

"I must try to change this balance of power." he thought, as he tried straightening his skeleton with a shrugging, rising up motion. His shoulder bones cracked as they were forced back to a more normal position from the contortion of the stress of this shaft. He felt weak.

"How long will I be here? Where am I going? Where am I?"

These desperate questions began running through his tired and frightened being. His weariness was not helped by the ache he also had in his head caused from the lack of complete vision and the worry of the dangers that might be about to occur.

With a glint of hope for reprieve from this place, he tried to slip mentally back into his other awareness, of his falling into the abyss. He was afraid. He wanted to recreate the circumstances that had possibly led him to this shaft place, so that he might escape the disorientation. But to where? Merm and the *Evil*? Suddenly he remembered the threat that was waiting there. He was perplexed. He was not sure of what to do, or what he could do. He questioned this place and how he had entered here. He began searching for some answer. Step by step he retraced his recent memory. It was most unclear as to how *recent*, his recent memory was. He noted for the first time that his sense of 'time' and its passing were now somehow different. He could no longer measure things in lines. It was not easy to place his thoughts or recent events into any meaningful sequence. Still, he tried the reconstruction. He began, with great effort, to see sections, or portions of thoughts and past events, though they were not being presented in a logical sequential order. He made allowances in his mind as best he could, so that he would have understanding of what he was seeing. It was hard, but he managed to create what he felt was a little order.

He concentrated. The last thing he could clearly remember was standing at the end of the Tunnel of Light after being ambushed by Lord

Merm and a Rider in the Cavern of Three in Tika. He remembered the fighting that ensued, and then how he had left the others in an effort to fulfill his destiny by making a dash for the only available escape. During his recalling of this memory, the discomfort of the shaft was forgotten. A spot in time opened and he was temporarily aware of being pulled again into another place, not physically but mentally. It was an odd sensation, very non sequitur. He had become an observer watching his memory off in the distance. He felt separated from his physical being, yet he was not. He was viewing himself and the other players of the memory that he had just recalled. They were on an elaborate stage. He watched as the memory played itself out.

Down he ran the length of the Tunnel of Light till he arrived at its opening.

"Where can I go?" There was nowhere to turn. From his vantage point he felt a duality. He was both watching and experiencing the scene with an eerie feeling that he was aware of the outcome, though not one hundred per cent certain, and partaking on the stage of all the emotions and dangers! He became bewildered. There was no escape. He was not safe. There was more than just the

players in this scene involved. There was a greater threat or Evil lurking. He found himself almost at the point of tears because of the conundrum he was in. A flash of a dream came to him. His father, —but how could that be. His father had been gone a long time now.

"How?"—There was no time to consider...

His father had told him what to do with the Key and the Passwords of Promise. Now that the Passwords had been delivered, all that remained was to properly dispose of the Key, as directed into the river from the Tunnel of Light. He found the action on the stage and the thoughts in his watching mind were faltering. There was a glitch, a hesitation. Something or one was cautioning.

"Should I throw the Key into the watery abyss? Is it safe?"

Julian was uncertain. That 'something' inside gnawed away at him. There was such vagueness in terms of thought and origins of feelings and events, that he almost sensed a repeat. It was as if this may not be the only time he had gone through this encountering. There was such a feeling of what might best be described as déjà vu, not of the events before him, but of the watching from this other place. Julian's mind was showing strain.

"Is this only a dream? Or is this, had this all really happened?"

Still he knew the time was not right. There was greater danger lurking by and he felt that as soon as he let go of the Key, that then it would be taken up by something, perhaps the Evil? He was not comfortable with abandoning the Key under such circumstances. There was also a feeling that the Key was his only way out. The sense of death that was amidst his intuitive being was his own. He knew that he had at this point of the scene reached an impasse.

"There is no way out! Or is there?"

Again the duality of thought. The confusion was irritating. There was no more logic. Everything was increasingly illogical in its presentation. He stood at the precipice full of fear in anticipation of an uncertain end. He was there and doomed, yet at the same time he was not, and though he could not project an outcome was, he believed, more safe. The choice to remain the observer, was a good one. Julian put more energy and singleness of mind into his role as the observer and not the performer who was about to be lost.

At the same instant that Julian was both watching and participating in these scenes he also became cognizant of Merm, who had quickly followed after him down the tunnel, having dealt with the others in the Cavern. These others involved were not yet recognizable, their faces and names were blurred in his mind. Though the thoughts were not truly complete in his watching, Julian understood that Merm was being propelled by the *Evil.* It was just an intuition.

"The Key must not now be lost to the abyss!" The words echoed through Julian as he ran up the Tunnel of Light in this re-enactment.

Merm followed and saw Julian come to a standstill. "The Southlander would be no match!" he thought as he began to smell the fear and indecision of the thief. He would be upon him in moments and then there would be an end to all of this.

How interesting that Julian as the watcher was also able to be a part of the role of the other characters on the stage. He was amazed by his ability *to be* Merm! Not entirely, but enough to feel a change of perspective within the memory.

It was as if all the emotions of the participants were available to him to experience. Julian was not able to comprehend the process by which this occurred, but it was happening. It seemed that the process of whoever or whatever was being focused upon in his mind, opened the way for Julian's absorption into the being of that moment in the memory. It was like sharing a consciousness; renting another's soul. It lasted until the focus had been fully explored or changed by some other distraction.

This renting or sharing came in glimpses and was interspersed with the other sharing. It was not of long duration these experiences of shared thought, just glimpses of the emotional background to the thoughts of those in the scene of the memory. There was no sentence structure or paragraphs, nor any organization to the communication. Each thought presented a myriad of choices, dilemmas, opportunities, resolutions, which all underlay the final resulting experience, directions of images, feelings and routes, which instantly were decided upon by the character in the memory. As soon as one path was taken, the whole confusion and contradiction of the analyses of the last choice ended, and the next began. It was enough to drive one crazy. There seemed no end to the process. As a watcher, Julian merely stole minute segments of all the experiences occurring, and continuing to occur before him, even when they were not traveling in concert with what was the apparent main direction of the scene within the memory, amidst all this confusion.

Julian's watching 'jumped', which seemed to be the best way to describe the process, of juxtaposition to the next sharing on the 'stage':

He was standing frozen in indecision at the end of the Tunnel of Light. He had no rational options left to him. He was caught. He could not go back up toward the Cavern of Three. He could never get past the large Gott, besides, even if he was able to somehow slip by, what about the others he would then confront? He knew that all of those in the cavern were not friendly or with his cause, and there was no time now to try and remember more about who 'they' were and whether he should take the chance. There was the wisp of a voice that he recalled just at the moment of his entering the tunnel. It was an old and Evil voice. He would not trust it, nor now could he allow Merm to capture him and acquire the Key. It wasn't even a matter of trust. Julian felt that he was linking with the object of the Key. It was a part of him and his destiny. He would not now let it go. If they were separated he would be overcome and lost.

"Use the Key to protect you both." Again there was a repetition of voicing. It was disturbing. There was only one path to follow!

As he saw Merm approach in the scene, Julian placed all his hope in the Magic. There was no more indecision. He committed himself to the images of the thoughts of what he felt was good. He was going on feeling. He didn't know what the impact of such thoughts might bring. Without realizing, he turned and with a confidence began to leap from the opening. There was an immediate slowing of motion in time. Every action was exploded into vastness. It was dreamlike. There was an expecting of a profundity of expression. It was the right choice and now Julian was about to embark upon a new territory. Then there was a jump back into the normal order and movements of what was Jard reality. As he prepared to leap, Merm had managed to arrive at the end of the Tunnel of Light just at the same instant *that Julian had made his choice to leap in faith. In trying to prevent the event, Merm who had misjudged his own speed and footing, managed to interrupt and speedily complete the action of Julian's decision of faith, by accidentally pushing, grabbing and then falling with him into the abyss. This came as a shock to both Merm and Julian. It awoke Julian from the confusion of his watching, jarring him back to a place and time he had just decided to leave. Turmoil set in once again. Angrily Julian turned in the direction of the intruder, and gave such a menacing scowl that Merm was taken aback and let go his grip of Julian's clothing. This reaction now astonished Julian as the two drifted about a length apart as they cut through the air on their way well into the abyss.*

The walls of the canyon sped by. They looked hard and ragged. The noise of the powerful river growing louder from below. The damp air clinging to their exposed skin. Every little aspect: touch, emotion, sight, sound, was being intensified. Things that normally would be ignored, were now paramount in importance to his questioning mind and senses. Every dimension of his feeling was noted. The world was turning inside out. The larger parts were dimmed and there was an imploding of awareness and a change from concreteness to the more abstract. The dangers of this world no longer existed or were of importance.

"What have I done?"

Julian could feel the fear of the events leading up to his 'leap', but had no perception of the danger that this abysmal fall presented to his person . He remembered as he witnessed in his mind the running approach of Merm from out of the blackness of the opening of the tunnel to the Cavern of Three, and then the sudden running into push and fall. It was an odd sensation. He was angry at the intrusion of this Gott upon his own choosing and method of leaping into the canyon abyss. There was really no fear, just annoyance. As he fell toward the bottom of the abyss which would soon lead into the Pass river and what would be instant death, he had gripped harder onto the Key out of an instinct. His attention was on the Key and his thoughts turned to hope.

"Father help me." he gasped, as he continued to fall. He felt an out of place lightness in his head and a rush of adrenaline throughout the rest of his body. He felt stimulated and alive as he turned and turned. He started to become dizzy, and without knowing why, he thrust out his arms above his head. The action of his arms was to stop his twisting as he flew. He pulled them back and began his tumbling. He threw out his arms again to stop the twisting. This time he kept them outstretched to remain more stable. The result of this stability allowed him to better view his surroundings and orientate himself. Merm was crying out after him, trying to claw his way through the length or so of the atmosphere that separated them both as they continued to fall. He hadn't learnt the lesson of stability and the more he waved about the faster he turned and twisted. For a moment it seemed like time was standing still, or maybe it was just the thrill of the free falling.

It seemed like an eternity had passed. Julian, still grasping the Key, considered his next steps—next steps!

"Why have I thought this? Is there a way out? Can I survive this?"

Many flashes went through his mind. Somehow he felt that he was becoming safe. Just like the river in his earlier experience. As long as he held the Key and focused upon the singular thought of hope he would be rescued from an otherwise terrible fate. The Key was meant to remain in his control a while longer, and he, survive this fall. His being went to a sense of duplicity. As he fell, he understood more and seemed to be becoming more, but he didn't know what. He felt different. More than just a Stoneman's son from Jard, with an obligation to protect this Key.

Ever since the incidence in the Cavern of Three and the unexpected intrusion by Merm he had felt unsettled. One moment he had understood everything, and then there had been a gradual muddling up of his thoughts. He seemed caught in between two identities. There was Julian of Jard, a persona he knew well, and then this other Julian, who just as he began to become acquainted with, was being lost to a mental fogging. The 'understanding' that he had clearly known in the Cavern of Three, was now very vague, and missing valuable sections. He was con-

fused, but amidst his confusion he still felt
that it was not the time to discard the Key.

"Merm is too close and the Key is not yet
safe from the Evil."

He heard these thoughts and realized that
his task was not yet completed. He remembered the tribulations of the journey thus far.
The dreams and the new awakenings, but the
last awakenings in the Cavern were becoming dimmed. Julian was drifting back to the
level of awareness of his first awakenings. It
all seemed bizarre. It would only be moments
and both he, the Key and Merm, would all
be below at the bottom! The quest would be
over.

The whole experience was one of change
and internal upheaval for Julian. He was
caught in the middle. A place neither here
nor there. A place of transition that operated
under completely new and bizarre rules. His
thoughts and moods kept switching from extreme to extreme. From knowing and understanding to not comprehending. During it all
there was a threat that kept him sane. He felt
that he was more, and would be again; that
he had hidden secrets that would reveal
themselves in time. He rationalized in one of

his normal moments that now was just not the time. This process continued. His consciousness jumped from extreme to extreme. Somehow he felt he was being manipulated but had no control, just awareness of that fact.

During the moments as he fell, Julian also considered other possibilities:

"Would Merm be able to work his way to him through the fall and manage to gain control of the Key before they crashed into the water below?"

Whether it was possible or not, this type of confronting thought soothed and brought a small amount of order to him as he watched his fall from this place. It did appear as if the Gott was getting closer. As long as this type of thought pattern helped to soothe, Julian decided to pursue that direction of thinking for as long as the calm would last. This process of rationalization brought his attention back to his immediate condition. He was suddenly aware of his sight and touch. Julian became aware and checked the reason for his clenched hand. He felt the Key. It was warm. It gave a slight tingling sensation against his palm. He tightened his grip in expectation of Merm's progression towards him.

Though Julian had no awareness of time, all was happening quickly! Each awareness and jump in his thought and experience within this shaft, was taking place in the smallest possible splits of time. He would not have believed the volume of passing phenomenon, if it were not actually happening to him. It was unfathomable. It was not possible! But it was happening. His lack of consistent and completed thoughts was growing progressively more maddening. The jumping from one to another memory episode distracting to the point of nausea. His mind wanted it to stop. To give up, or into, whatever was influencing his being and thought. He had lost all sense of place and order. He was losing the ability to determine whether he was in his world or in another. He was confounded by these new inward experiences.

This type of analysis of what might be externally occurring to him here was incorrect. It was based upon his ordinary rationalizations of the world of Jard. His assumption that what he was going through should resemble or become like his trained Jardian expectations of normal, and therefore explainable here, was naive. There would be no such clarification. The explanation would have to come from within Julian. There was no external causation to this experience and no comprehensible solution for him to act upon now. He was not ready to understand beyond his own self imposed limitations. He endured.

Soon, after no explicative remedy resulted, Julian accepted, that acclimatization to this experience of perception, was his best immediate solution. He was not yet skilled enough to know how to maintain his intellectual stability for long periods amongst this confusion. His use of the Magic was weak and limited to the realm of thought of his own world. He was in a place that he could not yet understand, though he was being affected. The fact that he had managed to maintain some sanity so far was based upon other powers, other benefactors. If he could manage to stay mentally afloat a little longer, then he might begin to interpret his intellectual and emotional turmoil.

Then without warning, his half conscious state changed. There was one part of him in this shaft-like place, and another in his own world. His attention shifted. He was in-between places. He was back in his awareness of his falling through the abyss. The noise of the surrounding passing air mingled with the distant power of the water below. It began to isolate his attention from Merm and their fall, to himself.

"What a strange sensation." Julian was no longer afraid of the impending death, but more the well being of the Key and the success of his obligation to prevent the Key from falling into the wrong control. "The Key must be protected!"

His thought turned to the underground passages near Norkleau, where he had been told all of this. His mind began replaying the memory of the event before him, as though it had just happened. It was such an odd sensation. He felt as if he had just gone through this type of experience, but could not quite place it. It was almost like déjà vu. Again, he was both watching and partaking in a replayed scene of a memory. It was more than just a dream, or a recalling of a past experience. He was again viewing from a distance. He was the only member of an audience, and it was being presented on a large stage before him. As it was being performed, he was becoming aware again of being more than just a passive member of the audience to this performance. He was also the actor. His awareness was split unevenly between watcher and performer.

For the first time this frightened him, his self control lapsed. There was no option but to watch and relive this memory of just a few sunrises before in the passageway near Norkleau Castle:

A dark silence wrapped about Julian. He was totally immersed in blackness. Paranoia gripped his being.

A panic set in. Had they just left or was it long ago. Julian sought the beam from the peep hole using it as a mental reference. He was awake not asleep. This wasn't a dream.

He could picture his face and body in his mind though it was impossible to see. Were his eyes opened or closed? He took his fingers to discover the truth. He told himself to get a grip on himself.

"JULIAN."

He held his breath, taking his mind off the ring in his ears that grew with each moment of silence.

"Julian."

There it was again!

"Julian."

"Who's there! Wha...wha...What do you want?! Whe...wher...Where are you?!"

"Julian, it is me."

"Keep away from me!"

The panic was immeasurable. Was this real or just his mind playing tricks.

"Julian," a glowing came out of the dark from above. Closer it came. Julian backed away till he could go no further.

"Don't be afraid my son," a holographic image formed from within the glow. Was he dreaming! He began to shudder with fearful apprehension.

"It is me, your father."

"Father?!" Julian's familiarity with the sound of the voice, slowly calmed him. He started to rise above the fear and ask more meaningful questions

"Father, is that really you?"

"Yes, boy. I'm here."

"Really, or is this a dream? Am I going mad?"

"No...you are not mad...I am here to help you. You must not tell the others that I came to you. What I have to speak of is only for the Stoneman's son. It is a part of our privilege for keeping the commitment. The commitment that has been passed on from son to son. The need has arrived. I am here to reveal the secrets that will be required to protect the Magic of the Old Ones that has been

left in our trust."

"You mean the Key?"

"Yes and more. There is powerful magic that the Key can unlock. It must not be permitted. It will only corrupt and unleash Evil in the Worlds. Misery and despair will live on forever. Only the Keepers of the Trust are immune to its lure. We are those Keepers."

"But why haven't you come before. All those times before?"

"The need is now. The Evil is awake and near. It is preparing to dominate the holder of the Key."

"But Merm has the Key. I don't see him giving in to anyone."

"It is out of his control. The Evil works with the greed, and corrupts the holder. We are the only ones who are incorruptible by the lure of its powerful magic. The Evil has no influence over us. We may use the Magic to protect and hide the Key from all others and thereby maintain the Balance in the Worlds. It is our entrusted obligation. You must use the Key to re-establish the Balance, and then return it to a place of safety."

"How will I do all that?"

"You will know at the time. A place is being prepared."

"By whom and where? What about the Balance?"

"When the Key is in your control, call upon the Magic to stop the Evil that spreads. It will respond only when it is assured of your capacity as Keeper."

"How will it determine my capacity?"

"You will know at the time."

"At the time! I should know now! I should be prepared."

"You are prepared. We have all been prepared for generations. There is no more to say."

"Don't leave. A moment longer please."

The image began a gradual fade.

"Father....Father....I love you...! Father!"

Before total disappearance a smile filled his father's face. Julian could not keep himself from weeping from the emotional realization of all that had occurred. Had it been a dream? Or had his father really been there conversing as if nothing had ever changed in their lives? Julian would not torment himself. He accepted all that had gone by. It was real in his thoughts. That was all that mat-

*tered. He looked to the peep hole to confirm
his wakefulness. The beam of light was still
pouring through. He was reassured.*

*How he had missed his father! It had been
so hard growing up through those critical
times, absent of a trusting male to give solace and support. He wondered how he had
managed to stumble to this age and seem so
strong and aware to others, but not to himself. How he wished he could be sure that he
was doing the right things; making the right
choices. How he wished he had had more
time to get the answers to all his childhood
fears and doubts. They had never entirely
left, but still held a grip on his soul. He was
in the dark, but not alone.*

All this had passed in an instant before him. It
made him wonder if he was about to die, since it
was said in Jard, that everything would pass before you when you were about to meet your
death. There was otherwise, no understanding the
reason, or what was responsible for triggering
this sudden recall. He searched his being for
some solution. He longed for an answer. He was
no longer afraid. This surprised him. His attention was drifting in and out, from the real, to
what he felt was imaginary. There was no time to

dwell on the approaching Merm through the air beside and behind in the abyss. Soon the water would determine the result of this chase.

As he searched his feelings for some explanation, Julian's thoughts of the water below triggered an emotional response.

"How I hate the water!"

He felt the shiver of the reminiscence of his submersion into the underground river on the way to Norkleau. It was cold and dark. The rush and pull of its current as he was sucked beneath into its power made a chill run down his spine. He was in its power. There had been a helplessness. His fate had been taken over by an alien strength, a strength that he was not sure of, but one he had managed to survive. He recalled that just as his breath was about to burst, he had arrived at the other side of the barrier that had blocked the above ground passage to Norkleau. He was suddenly breaking through the membrane of the control of the water, crossing back to his world and breathing air. Home, he was safe. He never wanted to go near water again. Especially this water.

"There is something more to this water, unlike the time in the water in Jard. This water has a presence. There is a silent entity within it."

Somehow he knew that the fluid was the skin that covered a rocky skeleton as it rushed through its many lengths and curves and falls. Julian was undecided as to the friendliness of this life within the water, and preferred not to confront it. He would be pleased to keep a respectable distance. As he fell, he dreaded the thought of death by the water.

From this thought his mind instantly turned to the second time he was lost to the power of the river on the way to Tika. He recalled the strength of its current again and his powerlessness amidst its pull. He felt the submersion and the strange sensation of a life within...again his control lapsed and the memory was replayed:

He was bobbing in the rough water of the river and gasping for air! Thodox and Quei were still running along the bank trying to keep pace with him. He would not last if he couldn't get to the bank soon. Every time his head went below the surface, it was longer till he popped back up. He can't die! Julian was being swept far away! Under he went again, and again and again...this last time he failed to surface. Julian was going down deeper. It was not right! The change in the river had been too sudden and Julian's ef-

forts should have been bringing at least some tiny result! A tremendous panic was taking hold. This shouldn't be happening!

When he had gone under and was held in place, preventing him from rising to the surface, a voice spoke clearly to him.

"Do not be afraid. It is the Evil that holds you. Take hold of the Key."

Julian fumbled to find the Key that he had tied into his pocket. Taking hold of it meant giving up one hand that might pull him to the surface. He trusted the voice and did what it had directed.

Julian had found the Key which was still where he had hidden it in his pocket. In using his arms to search, the force under the river completely overtook his body. He was being sucked deeper into its depths! He had taken hold of the Key in hope of some Magical rescue. None ensued. His breath was lean, and his mind was screaming out for fresh oxygen. Just when he thought he would explode, a voice was again present.

"Do not be afraid. Allow the moment to pass. You will not perish."

Julian had no other option but do as the voice beckoned. He relaxed and allowed his being to go limp.

"Think of the surface. Think of the bank."

He complied with the voice. He imagined that he was sitting on the bank on the other side of the narrows where the boulders were to allow the crossing. More and more he saw himself there. It was strange. The more he visualized himself actually there, the more comfortable he was in the water. His concern for fresh air was diminishing. This encouraged him to concentrate more till the only reality in his mind was of him on the other side of the river sitting on shore. It became more and more real. He closed his eyes. More and more he imagined the scene. Soon he did not even hear the muffled sound of the water all around him, or even its feel. He concentrated further. He actually began to hear the cool night breeze and feel the air blowing against his wet body. He thought to open his eyes, but was afraid to break the vision, his only hope of relief!

He kept this up for what seemed a long time. Finally, he could not withstand the temptation to see where he had been pulled by the river. He opened his eyes—he was sitting on the bank on the other side of the river! He patted himself to check if it was a dream. It was real! Somehow the magic within the Key had saved him!

This vision was interrupted by Julian's thought. He once more focused his attention, which had jumped itself back from the thoughts of Merm and their falling through the abyss, and onto the two incidents within the river. There was so much disarray in his thinking process. Jump and jump and jump. His mind was in a state of juxtaposition. The speed of the jumps seemed to be increasing and he felt that he was about to be overcome by an overpowering visual, emotional and intellectual barrage. He persisted in holding, as long as he could, onto one consistent linear thought.

As the memory jumps threatened, he struggled to hold onto the reality of both of those times in the river, with his remembrance of its strength and personality. He began to analyze those thoughts and recall:

"While in the river there had been something other than the fear and panic! Why had I not paid much heed to this before?"

He had felt something other than the wet and cold. There had been a presence! Both times there had been a voice, calming and protecting.

Both times there had been the Key. His mind was repeating the same thoughts, but becoming narrower in focus. He was not sure where he was.

"I must continue to hold the Key. Holding the Key would save me. I must concentrate upon the Key...the Key...the Key!"

Julian was no longer in a state of understanding. He was mentally and spiritually separate. He was in a state of perfection within a nothingness, a between place which needed an imperfection to give impetus to direction. He was on a metaphorical bridge in time and space, which spanned what is, to what isn't, or what could be, to what should be. His being screamed out for substantive corroboration.

"Who is guiding me? Where am I?" His nothingness mesmerizing. He was in a phase of metamorphosis, but into what?

The sound of the rushing air and the crying out of Merm further diminished as Julian transferred his attention more and more upon his grip on the Key from his growing state of nothingness. His mind was gradually containing no other thought. He felt as if a powerful drug was beginning to overwhelm him. Strangely he was beginning to feel more secure in this situation. It was a feeling he did not want to lose, and so, as an addict would do, devoted his will more and more upon the source of the safe feeling and the pleasure it gave, till gradually there was no other reality other than the pleasure of the safety within his conceptualization. There was otherwise so much uncertainty and confusion.

All of this process had been accomplished within the few instants of the pushing and falling from the opening of the Tunnel of Light into the abyss to the river below. The harder Julian concentrated upon the Key in his grasp, the faster the separation occurred in his mind between his present peril and the safety he so desired. There was no choice on Julian's part in which direction his thoughts should follow. Whether he survived or not, an instinct from deep within was directing his course. He no longer attempted to resist this silent direction, though he was not fully aware of its source. The memories of the river and his previous salvation spurred him on. It was not a rational thing that he did, rather irrational. As before in the river, he just began to let himself go into and along with the nothingness; to ignore the pressing dangers of the real world and solely rely upon the security of the power of the not real. Julian was very confused and disoriented. He was not sure anymore what was real and what was imaginary. Perhaps they were both *real* in their own sense. Perhaps the separation between the two was an artificial one placed there by someone or thing to add a sense of order to an already busy universe! His mind jumped to visual replay of his memory of events at the Cavern of Three. Julian in a daze, watched himself:

...step unto the dais. He took the Passwords of Promise from their hiding place in his cloak. Untying the twine that bound them together, he moved forward and peered down into the coffin.

'The Keeper,' he thought. He knelt before the edifice and mumbled indistinguishable words that were half melodic in sound. When he had finished, he turned his head to show a smile. He felt reassured that he could continue and complete the task. He rose up and placed the books gently amongst the bones that were once a hand. Remarkably the bones held together as he touched them. They seemed to rise up a little and seemed to grasp hold of the Passwords.

After they had been placed, Julian backed away a step. He stood still for a moment. He then removed the Key from its hiding place in his clothing. Holding it up in front of his forehead with his right hand, he presented it to the Keeper. The chant of old began:

"Ic noon vra ba, houn gre juk!"

It was in the oldest tongue. The language of the Old Ones. The Stoneman found himself watching from outside his body as others controlled, or shared their essence within him. He was not afraid. He knew it was meant to be. It was all part of the calling as a Stoneman and a Keeper of Three. He watched as he chanted. There began a deep rumbling in the cavern. A voice shouted:

"Go! With the Key!"

Julian knew he must hurry. He turned to check the books that he had placed within the bones. They were gone! All that remained were ashes, but they weren't the ashes of the books! There was no time to consider. He turned and ran into the tunnel that housed the shaft of light.

These were unfamiliar thoughts for Julian to possess, and he wondered at their sudden apparition, especially now! He pondered more and more upon them. He considered more and more the dilemma between real and imaginary. He became more perplexed and lost his conscious ability to continue within this unexplored area of his understanding. He felt elevated and alive. He felt as if he were on the verge of knowing some great discovery, but was incapable of communicating or relegating language and linear concepts to the experience. It was as if the real world existence and experience of Jard were preventing him from acknowledging any other existence possibilities. He was like a newborn exposed without choosing, to a brand new foreign place. A place that operated upon a completely divergent and almost totally unrelated set of rules or understandings. He had suddenly been immersed into this turmoil of thought, a turmoil he felt he was not ready to be in, yet he knew it was his only choice. There were such contradictions. He had a sense of intuitive awareness, but the language to successfully or completely communicate or express the experience eluded him. He knew the basics, but only on a survivalist tactile and emotionally confused level of understanding. He felt dependent upon unknown conventions and powers that could both hurt and help him. Ignorance was now his captor. Though he was unwilling, he was succumbing to this master.

♀ ♪ ♪ ♪ ♪ ♪ ⸮ ☰ ∿⌒ ☞ ☞

"Shruu jik doi!" came Lenore's voice
followed by her own pulse of three
narrow beams of multicolored light
emanating from her arms and wrists. Each struck
within the cloud. After each striking, there came
from deep inside the cloud, a groan of pain,
followed by a grumble of anger.

"You have caught me off guard with your
trick," the voice snarled from the cloud, "but
have missed your mark. Now I will see you
squirm! You will soon beg for death!"

With that there followed an uninterrupted exchange of power between the two. Lenore, who
was still invisible to sight, was being tracked

through the Magic by the *Evil*. Flash followed flash. The whole dream was filled with brilliant colors from the powerful beams being hurled about.

The sleeping Lenore watched all of these events from within her dream. She was unable to awaken. She could not speak to, nor direct the imagery. It was as if she were split into two distinct personalities: one watching from a safe distance and the other involved in the action. Though they both shared a complete empathy within the dream, she was distanced from actual involvement or suffering. What was more unsettling was that something other than the *Evil* of this cloud had a grip on her from within the dream. It would not let go. It was pulling her towards something of great old knowledge. Lenore was afraid to divert any of her sleeping attention for even the slightest moment, from her concentration of the present fight, in order to discover more about this other thing that was pulling, or rather calling, to her. She felt that if she did, it would provide an opportunity, a weak spot, of which the *Evil* would most assuredly take advantage. Then, she believed, she would be doomed. Her physicalness would be lost, and she would be adrift. She knew if this happened, that she would then never wake again, worse still, the fate of her 'boys' would then certainly be sealed. Somehow she sensed they were still alive and that she was playing an important role in securing their safety by engaging this entity of the cloud. Lenore had no choice but to continue watching from within the imprisonment of her dream. Each moment seemed to last forever.

She was amazed by what she viewed. Her personage in this dream was very beautiful, a beauty that Lenore had never noted. It radiated from her. It was not the beauty of the skin, nor was it young. It was very, very old, older than possible. It was as if there was another Lenore in this scene. She was attached to the sleeping female but greater. The woman in the dream was the physical, but her sleeping person spiritual. It was odd. In the dream 'that' Lenore held great abilities that 'this' Lenore had never before considered. She marveled again at how they both were contradictorily but intimately joined together.

During all of these revelations, the fighting had continued. The emotions of the experience were as overpowering for this simple Jardian female, as was the fight in which she was engaged. Lenore was still invisible in the dream, but her sleeping body could see her. The fight was hard. Gradually the *Evil* was gaining in strength, and pushing Lenore back. Back to someplace out of visualization. Lenore wondered where she was being pushed. Then, out of the emptiness of her dream appeared a great canyon. The *Evil* was backing her to its ledge. With this realization, Lenore became visible within the dream. The drain to her strength, caused by all the stress, was growing. She stumbled and fell, landing at the canyon's cliff ledge. Turning her view from the cloud, she quickly reconnoitered. It was a great abyss with a river at its bottom.

The *Evil* sensing the sudden shift in power, shot another beam at Lenore and advanced. Lenore, still lying upon the ground, threw her arms together to shield her, as she attempted to muster more of her own energy through her fingers, to counter its approach. She began to feel doomed.

"I will not give up! I will take you over with me." Lenore was slowly losing ground, but she was still locked together in combat with this *Evil*. They had a strong grip on each other. The dream was so real. She could feel and hear the noises as she was being pushed slowly along the ground toward the edge.

"Wrik loo no my trd pir!" this had unexpectedly come from her, along with a powerful burst of a beam which hit and jarred the *Evil* back. It was strong but it did not deter it. In response it shot back a beam toward her, driving her to where one more attack would push her over the ledge and into a terminal fall.

Lenore was on the verge of tears as she watched herself loosing hope of a win. What could she do to help her dream personality? How could she help prevent this fate? Her boys needed her. Where could she turn? She thought for a moment and then *there...there* was the answer!

2

Nothingness. Everything seemed to be pointing toward contradiction and a blankness. There were no words to adequately describe or define anything here in this state. Julian found himself grappling for some 'reason'. A meaning. A beginning, middle and end. He was still a product of his logical Jardian thinking world. He required a linear explanation. He searched as his conceptualization remained under attack by whatever, wherever, or whenever he was. His thought drifted to his youth. To a similar time of misunderstanding and a thirsting for answers to impossible questions. To the most simple of questions of: beginnings, middles and endings.

His parents had been humble simple folk, though he could only barely remember his mother. His only lasting record of her was one more of empathy than concrete physicalness. He felt her warmth, her loving glow. He saw her eyes—eyes that showered with a joy and a passion of living. This was the imprinting of an infant bonding with its partner of birth and survival. These were the only strong memories he had of her, though he had always felt her nearness during the years since her passing. He did not remember her actual passing. He had still been an infant. Nothing was ever said on the subject in his home by his father, who was a very stoic hard working individual, nor by any in his family, or friends in Jard.

When Julian had grown to that age of inquisitiveness he asked many questions. These questions were cleverly avoided, or he was simply told that she was gone and that nothing, including questioning, would bring her back. After a time he stopped asking the questions, but inside he had always wondered.

This wondering was gradually replaced with the larger questions to which his young unsatisfied mind went. From queries on birth through death. From beginnings to endings. There had been an endless amount of uncertainties through which the young Julian needed guidance. The passing of his mother had created a void early in his life. A void that needed filling. He recalled the one time that his father had broken the pattern of his usual avoidance of Julian's never ending queries on life, and had attempted to bring some order to his son's shaping mind.

It was in the spring, in Jard. The son had gone to spend the day working and learning the craft of the stone at his father's workshop. It was a lovely early spring morning. Julian was watching, as his father was choosing the stone slabs that were to be used in a new structure to be built in Jard. They were in the storage yard behind the shop. Everywhere there were huge rectangular and square chucks of stone all lined up by size and shape in this back space. Some were so large that they appeared like small mountains to Julian. He entertained himself while his father measured and checked calculations for the job, by climbing these 'mountains'. He was carefree and happy, and a little bored.

The workshop was located on the southeastern part of Jard, which was a short distance from their home on the southwest side of the village. This part of the community was the area of the craftsmen's shops and larger workspaces. It was still very quaint, but not as picturesque or as well kempt as the rest of Jard. It was here that the many trades people prepared and stored their work, which eventually was used by the rest of the community to create and maintain the beauty of Jard.

His father's workshop was not large. There was a big window on the front, and the entrance to the structure was on the western side, through the gate of a sturdy stone wall that stretched around the perimeter of the property. The shop had been in the family since the beginning of his family's life in Jard. It was a quaint place, though not tidy. There were slabs of all types of stone from all the Worlds sitting and waiting in the backspace until their moment of glory arrived, the moment when the stonemason would awaken the beings that lay frozen within the stone. The Stoneman would release and make them more than just chucks of stone. He would give them purpose and life.

Julian was sitting up to the right side of his father, upon a small square slab. His father was running both his eye and hands over another larger rectangular slab about three lengths away. Julian was bored. He wanted to do something. He found the process of 'spending the day' with his father at work, not as exciting as he had at first believed it would be, when it had been suggested to him at dinner the night before. He had somehow expected his father to do much more exciting things. He wanted to change the sameness of his day so far. From out of his boredom, Julian half heartedly posed a question, as his father examined the stones.

"What is nothingness?"

Julian had been playing with his friends the sunrise before, and they had begun to try and imagine nothingness. They had all been unable to understand their inability to do such a thing, since even imagining nothing was something. This set up a quandary in their young minds which had been mulling in Julian's unusually inquisitive mind ever since. Though his friends had laughed and moved on to other more immediate thoughts at the time, Julian was suddenly immersed in all the possibilities posed by such a questioning. There had been so many possibilities. He needed some help. He was thinking more out loud from his boredom, never expecting that his father would notice or respond, or that he would just be told not to think on such things as was usual.

Julian's father, upon hearing the question stopped his work, and turned his glance directly up to his son. Julian, who was playing with some stone dust in his hands, suddenly felt the gaze and looked down directly into his father's eyes.

His father was motionless. The two became connected. Julian had been asked to explain his question, and he had. What followed was an unexpected conversation. Julian was speaking with his father as an equal for the first time. The explanation had been in the terms and imagery that a stonemason would use.

His father began by pointing out the variety of stones in the backspace. He had asked his son what he saw.

"Nothing." Julian's answer had been innocent.

"Nothing?" had come his father's response. Julian now replayed part of the old memory:

"Nothing? Really? There is much more. From these stones will come great accom-

plishments. Within each is energy and magic. There is no such thing as nothing." He drew Julian's attention to the area of the workspace that housed the work in progress. "Do you see nothing there?"

Julian answered that the other stones were uncompleted work.

"But they are or were just a short time ago 'nothings'. How can they be nothing and something?"

Julian was getting confused.

"Think of it this way, there is always something. Even from nothing. You should think of nothing as only the absence of direction. One day a tool starts a chip in the stone, and then the 'nothing' embarks upon a direction, becoming something; having meaning in time and space where before it had none. It is from that spark, that the whole process begins. Nothing is a state of symmetry. A perfect symmetry, waiting for chance or design to create imperfection. From that imperfect state we have created all this."

It had been a short conversation, after which his father, noting Julian's bewilderment, had shrugged and told him to come along. There was much more work to do before they would return home. Off they both went to the shop. Not another word was said with regard to Julian's question, nor did the son pose another. He was in a state of bewilderment. For the first time in his life, his father had shared as an equal. Julian walked more erect and proud. He felt that his father was becoming his friend.

For many years since that conversation Julian had contemplated his father's attempt at explaining nothingness. Since that day Julian had begun to think differently upon it.

'A perfect symmetrical state.' "What did father mean?"

Julian had examined the concept and had begun to realize the beauty and simplicity of the explanation. He had tried to imagine the state of existence which he might consider to be the nothingness at the beginnings of time. Here, according to his father's explanation everything would be in a state of perfect symmetry. There would be no discernible differences and certainly no change. Everything would be merely existing and constant. Change was the key. The question of what caused or created that change was not important. It could have been merely accidental or a result of a knowledge not available to those of this 'directional' world. What was important was that something had forced a change from which there could be a measurement. Over the duration of the change, or 'time' by our conceptualization, this world was created.

The part of this perfect symmetry that was affected, might be large or small. In fact, there were probably other parts of the symmetry that were affected by other causes and moving in their own directions, equally ignorant of us, as we them. Our world, our concepts, our measurements were different from that of any other change occurring within the perfect symmetry. Nothingness was static and uneventful. There was no direction or change. It was a state of perfection in the universe.

"But what created the nothingness?"

It was clear that the problem was Julian's question. For his question was burdened by the limits and thinking of his world's creation; his world's arrogance. His thinking was a product of his world's experience and all those before in this changed 'direction'. The need to describe and explain in terms of that direction was understandable, but in the greater picture, meaningless. His world's direction was just as probably accidental, as planned. Even the concept of 'planned' was egocentric and of his world's thinking. It would be hard to imagine that there were no universal beginnings that would be acceptable to his thinking or experience. For from his world there had been a creation, and 'time' was the measurement of that change from the 'beginning' to the present 'position'. This type of time measurement was linear and part of his world's direction, but was not necessarily representative of any other directions or changes to the symmetry. It was certainly inapplicable to any non linear events and directions that existed along other changes to the symmetry of the nothingness.

Julian was surprised at his thinking on these thoughts. They were bizarre in their timing. He was falling into an abyss where his demise was close, and yet, he was contemplating all these memories. Though he knew that the atmosphere he was falling through would soon end in a very concrete way, in his thoughts he was not afraid. He wondered what could trigger this new safe awareness. He was beginning to understand something. There was a new direction to his pattern of thought. He was beginning to find an awareness, a completeness, a certainty within himself that was new to him. There seemed to be a beginning oneness with something greater than himself. He no longer felt like a victim of whatever was the cause of his thought directional change from one beginning perfect symmetry to another. He was no longer a prisoner being forced to fulfill this abysmal destiny, but instead a passenger. A willing passenger with choices. It seemed to Julian, as he fell through the abyss and remembered, that he was merely to alter his choices and he would no longer be in this predicament of falling to his death. The questioning that he had always had, was becoming silent. He needed to center his awareness on something else.

All of the thoughts that were running through Julian, were coming from deep within his being. There was no conscious control on his part. There appeared to be other factors at work now. Somehow the jumping and the gripping of the Key had ignited others within him. He was at a crossroads in time. He felt as if he was able to open a door and step from here into another direction where he could be safe from danger. Suddenly he had a momentary glimpse of the Magic. In a flash he was totally aware of all that had gone before. He knew that he must take another leap forward in his mind. That he must open the approaching door that was metaphorically being presented to him.

It was at this time of understanding. At the precise moment of single awareness, the step between where only one of the directions of the Worlds exist, and another begins, that Julian's consciousness changed. His physicalness demanded a choice of awareness. In a momentary blinding light and flash, Julian had chosen a different direction of thought. A new direction that he was not very cognizant. After this choice was made, Julian propelled himself back into confusion.

Julian's moment of knowing had allowed him to cross into the direction that led to the Magic, though he still was not aware of this fact. All he perceived was the chaos that was within his mind. He was not conscious of any influencing on his part, of his situation. He was no longer viewing memories or jumping from image to image. Now, he was merely feeling safe. The danger or threats were gone. Merm, the canyon abyss, the river, and the falling had suddenly vanished, and Julian was no longer falling into the abyss. He was, instead, falling through the circular shaft, and not down into the abyss. His consciousness was no longer split between existences. He was completely back in the shaft place. He was now able to explore it more thoroughly.

The shaft was vaguely circular and only large enough in diameter to allow the passage of someone or thing, about his own size. There was a glowing within it, from multicolored particles which together grouped and formed its circular shape. Julian was dumbfounded by the beauty of the sparkling particles. He was being transported by them and was in a constantly shifting motion. He assumed this by the way he was being tossed about within its confines.

Beyond the shaft's luminescent particle circumference there was still 'nothing'. A complete darkness in every possible direction, as far as he could see. Once he focused his thought upon this motion, he began to question if he was moving, or if it was the sea of black around him that was in motion. He decided it was himself in the shaft. As he moved along, it seemed as if the way behind him, which was only a length or so away, closed down into blackness, after his passing through, and a newer opening out of the blackness ahead opened. It was as if he was within an elliptical bubble of some sort traversing this place enroute to some predetermined destination. No, it was not a bubble. It was more like a shifting shaft that gradually allowed its passenger to move swiftly through the darkness of this place; a place illuminated only by the shaft of light.

His attention changed. He began to feel a tingling throughout his body and a growing sense of strength. A strength that he had also noticed previously when he had been rescued from the water of the Pass River en route to Tika. He surmised that something within this glowing shaft was influencing his senses. He allowed his being to go along with his feelings and decided to observe whatever he could. It was a strange place. It reminded him of a labyrinth, twisting and turning, and never knowing exactly where you were going.

As he progressed he thought he noticed other shafts coming and going in every which way around his own shaft, momentarily shedding light beyond the darkness. A light that was quickly swallowed up by the void. It was impossible to get any directional bearings or idea of distances covered; even time itself had lost any meaning of measurement to him here. He tried to glimpse the contents of the various appearing and disappearing shafts during their quick passing, hoping that they would reveal something, though he wasn't sure what that might be or what purpose it would serve. He was not able to see if there were other passengers in these shafts. As he strained to see, he considered for a moment the impact that the whole setting was obviously having upon him.

This place was awesome and distracting. There seemed to be something new at every corner of this spherical place. Other than the brief flashes of the light from a shaft before it vanished back into the blackness from which it had just as quickly entered, there was no other sign of life. He was the only corporal being in this place. Gradually he gave up waiting for, and trying to view inside the other shafts. He turned his attention inward to his own traveling environment and began to feel alone.

Everything here was foreign. The shaft was not made up of definite sides, but rather obtained its shape from the particles, which seemed to be forces of some type of energy. He reached out with his right hand and attempted to push it through and into the void. The farther he went, the farther the multicolored energy glowed. There was no way to go beyond its protective envelopment. It clung to him no matter how forced the movement. There was no pain involved in this glove like covering. There was no sensation other than an increase in the tingling he felt throughout his whole body. The farther Julian attempted to move into that which lay beyond, the stronger the tingling became. No harm to his hand was experienced. This, he assumed, was protection to possibly the danger of being in the void and not within a shaft. He did not know if it was possible to survive out there, but reasoned that his present situation within the shaft was for safety, not imprisonment. He did not account for this conclusion further, being too enthralled by the phenomena. He played games and teased with the energy glow for a short time by moving his hand back and forth, in and out, humored by the changes within the sensation.

After the novelty had worn off, Julian tried to call out, but no sound came forth. There was no sound! Funny, he had not really noticed this silence before since he was busy in his examination of the shaft. He now became acutely aware of the absence of any sound whatsoever in this place. His focus of observation shifted from the visual and tactile to the realm of sound and vibration. He put his palms over his ears and rubbed them, trying to clear away any blockage that there might be around his ears preventing him from hearing, but there was nothing, not even the sound of his touching. He could feel the touch to the skin of his outer ear by his rough hands, but not the scratching sound that should have been present. He best compared the sound to that of a large lake shell, the type that could be found near the shores on the Lake of Choices. He remembered those times well.

As a child Julian often journeying there with his father on trips to purchase new stone. He recalled his joy at finding and then placing the large shells, that no longer housed any creature, next to his ear, listening to the distant roar that came from within their spiral shape. It was a sound that could be created with the covering of his hands over his ears as well. This sound was the one that he had expected to hear now.

Satisfied that his ears were not blocked and that there was nothing else wrong with himself, Julian concluded it could only mean there wasn't any sound or noise here. He became acutely aware of the absence. Not even the internal sounds of his own body as his blood rushed through his veins and his breathing tumbling through his windpipe and into his lungs, could be heard. A sharp pang of fear went through him. He tried to get a grip on the panic that was swelling within this silent world. He was being confronted with so many terrifying changes.

After some moments, he wondered if the lack of sound was to be permanent, or just a passing event. The only sound he could hear was the unspoken words of his own thoughts. He lay back and starred mindlessly into the void. He watched as he continued to fall / travel through this place not knowing what to do or expect next. It reminded him of his experience in the underground river on the way to Norkleau, where he was ushered along without any control. He was a captive of the water's strength with its own unannounced purpose.

More moments passed. On and on he went in the shaft. He could see no end, but knew there must be one. It seemed as if he had come this way once before. His journey through the underground river had perhaps given him a glimpse of things to come, but this place was different. He had no *real* recollection of such a place as this void and shaft of light in his experience. It was more terrifying here. Even the river had had sound. Sound that had reassured him of his being, and his place within his own universe. He could handle many things, but the loss of sound unnerved him. — Sound! How strange to be affected this way. He could not remember a time when he had been so afraid. Afraid? It was unusual and he felt it was unbecoming of a Stoneman and Keeper. It was not their way. He must overcome this in order to survive the challenges that he knew would be ahead, and did not yet understand if he was ever to find a way out of this place. He felt like an infant as he remained protected and held within this shaft. How he would welcome any sound!

He tried to change his thoughts in an attempt to regain some security. His mind was jumping from image to image each with its own emotional impact. It was not of his control. With the absence of vibrator experience his brain wandered in search of other sensorial absences that he may have overlooked. As it wandered, he became aware of another absence—time. There was no longer any idea of time. He had lost all concept of the duration and passage of events.

With the barrage of non linear thoughts, images and emotions that had been upon him, he realized that there was no way to measure where in time all these things had and were taking place. There was no pattern that could be established.

"Was this nothingness?" he thought. No, he was in motion towards something, he felt this inside, therefore this was not the perfect symmetry, and as such there had to be time. Julian concluded that it must be appreciated differently in this place, not measurable or comprehensible as his linear world, which he surmised was somewhere out there in the void. This distress, and the lack of any sound, was confusing his orientation. He appreciated how much he was slave to those two aspects of his world. He was amused by the notion of whether he had been, and was master of his direction, or merely a viator trammeled by a combination of sound and his concept of linear time. Perhaps it was all just a game and he didn't really exist at all! He was being played with by other beings, for whom he was providing entertainment.

Julian was flabbergasted. The absurdity of this line of thinking was obviously a sign, in his estimation, of his tiring under the strain of his present circumstances. He missed the tranquillity of before he had entered here. He longed for re-attachment to the *other* world from which he assumed he had come, though he still wasn't sure how he had stumbled into this shaft or place.

Everything was upside down and inside out. He imagined himself to be caught in-between somewhere. A thin sliver of a place that was slicing through eternity. He did not believe that this place was in his *other real* world, nor in another world, though he could not determine the origin of this 'knowing'. This was a separate and different universe. There was a haunting quality to it. No dangers presented themselves. He was not in a state of fear for his safety, but rather confused on what to expect next. He knew that this was a safe place and that he was, at least momentarily, out of the reach and harm of Lord Merm and any other *Evil*. Somehow he had fallen into this shaft, and not understanding the how or why, was unsettling to him.

It was so hard to convey what was happening to his mind, to express or make any sense of the irrational placement of images and emotions that were assaulting him. There was so much juxtapositioning in everything that had elapsed or been presented since his entry into the shaft, that putting it into some reasonable or usable order was impossible. So many incredible things were passing before his sight, he did not linger long in his thoughts on any other place that may or may not exist. He rationalized that it was all beyond his present control and that he should pay more heed to his immediate needs.

It was at this moment that Julian began suddenly to feel assured. He felt a compulsion to let go of his other consciousness of his other world and all the meanings attached to his life and dwelling there. His other reality would not help him here. He must allow this new birth here to conceal and consume him. He would deal with the *other world* when the need arose. Now he must learn more! There was a purpose for his being here!

His mind drifted to a replaying of a memory from his past. It was different from his other memories. This time, as Julian was watching the dream, everything was in distortion and slow motion. He watched. He felt the shiver of a sweat of terror, as the voice in the memory called out to him in a strange language, the language of the Old Ones:

"Nik, wroo bien ha! Nik, wroo bien ha! Nik, wroo bien ha!" There was a desperate look upon his face. He thought it was pleading for something.

The scene was from a distance and hard to identify but gradually Julian could make out the trees as Moonfruit. It was dark all around and he could feel the damp of the night. This was taking place in the Burning Forest. The figure was backing away from something, something awful and powerful or so he thought. Julian could feel the presence, but not see a thing other than the forest as a backdrop to this retreating individual. He had no idea who it was.

"Nik, wroo bien ha! Nik, wroo bien ha! Nik, wroo bien ha!" was called out to him, even more pleading and desperate. Was it a warning of some kind?

As the sequence persisted there was a sudden forceful move of his location and angle of view. Julian was now seeing a close up of the scene. He could now only see the back of the figure. He could see its outstretched hand at first pointing away then directly at him. Julian was fixed upon the hand, everything else became a blur. It was old and wrinkled. It was ugly and bony. The skin like ancient sun abused leather. Big dark spots, or growths were leaching on to the skin. He was being drawn closer and closer. It was becoming more uncomfortable to watch. He closed his eyes but the scene did not diminish from his sight. The blur began to clear. Julian could venture a timid gaze away from the pointing hand. He could make out a dark cloak. There was a hood. It was loosely fitted and concealed the face. The whole recalling was becoming more and more horrific. This was not a friend it was...!

This sequence abruptly ended. Julian was panting and his shirt was wet from his apprehension. He was safe. He was in the shaft. His eyes were wide open. He was watching and waiting for whatever was to follow. This last memory had been just as real as his others, but this time more prophetic. He tried to imagine where it had come from within his experience, but could find nothing that even closely resembled it. Reluctantly, he considered the possibility of it not being his memory at all! Could it have been a vision of things to come? There came unpredictably another memory jump. Julian was thrown into a brief moment of another image of which he again had no memory of his own. He could see a strange blue gray cloud billowing from the center of his view:

"Get out!" He felt cold and shivery, and began to growl out words to something he felt was there threatening, but not yet visible:

"Get out! ...Ici Ni Ban yi."

He heard himself uttering these strange words; they were in the language of the Old Ones. He wasn't sure what they meant, but knew they were words of power. He switched *back to his own tongue, "**Get Out!**..." Then a series of tremendous multicolored beams all hitting and absorbed into the opaque cloud appeared out of nowhere.*

The image and memory ended. He remained still. 'Please no more' was spoken but not heard. Julian lay exhausted by the intensity of the memory jumping, as his journey through the passage carved by the shaft, continued. He was drained. He would never have predicted that such an experience as this could ever have happened to him. He marveled at his capacity to remain at least somewhat composed. He had not gone mad, nor given up contact with his deepest being. It even seemed that he was getting used to being here.

Julian turned his mind to his perspiratorily uncomfortable feeling, and mentally inventoried his physicalness. His body was tense. There was no harm to him other than the strain, and his nervous sweat. There was an object in his hand. It was the Key! He had forgotten that he had the Key and upon its rediscovery, began to remember where he had come from and why. Perhaps this had been his saving grace. He noted the security that the holding of the Key, which was solidly in his hand, gave. He began to recall an awakening within himself, just before he had fled down the Tunnel of Light and into the jump that had somehow brought him eventually here. But the memory was not as clear as he felt it was before. He had sensed another presence, but now it was gone. It was being submerged. He was so very confused, but one realization was still strong: amongst all the uncertainties and questions one fact remained certain—the Key. The Key would protect him. He knew this without doubt. It was his ally and had brought him away from the threats that followed. He did not question this truth. Just as he had trusted the grasping of the Key in the river, now he trusted again. It was an ancient knowing.

During all that had occurred since his leaping into the canyon abyss, there had been a clutter of emotion, thought, and imagery, in his being. He had been thrown back and forth between complete awareness, to total ignorance of all his memory, abilities, and awakenings. He was no longer heading in a definite direction, or to his thinking, purpose. He felt numb, as if he had just survived an intense brainwashing. There were many questions he would like to pose to someone, anyone. The undeniable fact that he was in this strange place, was the only evidence to himself that he was dealing with powers, and magic beyond the world of Jard. If he had ever doubted the existence or truth of the lore of his father's stories, the journey here had now finally erased such foolishness, making him born again within the Magic. Though this place was disorienting, Julian was here for a purpose.

"The Key." he confidently said the words. No sooner than he had had this moment or realization, it disappeared. He was left again in his uncertainty and ignorance.

The time, if that existed here, passed. Julian noted the sameness as he traveled. He was heading somewhere, but he did not know where it was, or when he would arrive. He did know he would find many answers once there. His thoughts turned from fear and panic, to adventure. He found himself welcoming whatever lay ahead; if the direction he was moving toward was 'ahead'! He was relieved to be away from his pursuers. But was he? A concern awakened in him. "Perhaps *they* would follow!" The panic was again alive. He must continue his flight and discover the place he was to hide the Key. He must escape from the *Evil*! Another memory jump possessed him:

He saw himself in the Cavern of Three. He

was checking for the Passwords of Promise that he had placed within the bones of the Keeper. They were gone! All that remained were ashes, but they weren't the ashes of the books! There was no time to consider. He was turning and ran into the tunnel that housed the 'shaft of light'. The Evil was near! From somewhere a voice commanded to someone:

'Go after him. Get the Key!' Stop the one with the Key! He must not let the Key go!'

How did he know of the shaft of light?

And then everything in his mind went blank for a moment. The image ended. Julian jumped back to the only consistency he knew here: the shaft of light and the Key. The Key. The Key had been at the center of everything. He was linked to its magic. He was protected. He thought of his first introduction to the magic of the Key. It had been in the underground passageway at Norkleau. Julian was waiting for someone to bring him the Key. He wasn't clear in this memory on anything but himself and the Key. Out of the blackness of the Norkleau passageway had come a voice that was familiar to him. He wondered at his present difficulty to identify or see the face that belonged to the sound. The memories were changing. There was less general detail, but more specific itemization within the scenes. By now he understood not to struggle with the jumping within his mind, but to simply allow the process to pass. He hoped it would be a brief experience. He watched as the memory unfolded:

"Uncle J!" called out the voice.

Julian looked in the direction of the sound and shortly a torch light became visible. He strained to see.

"Whose there?" But there came no response. Then out of the dim torch light came a hand and the voice:

"Here's the Key. Please hurry.

"Don't worry little one," Julian's voice was stranger than normal, "all will be fine. I know what to do. Follow me. Do not let me be prevented from my path."

Next Julian saw himself pushing on a rock wall within the underground passage. It was a different location than where he had been given the Key. In the recalling he had jumped from there to here. The rock wall moved. It was a door of rock! After the entrance was opened, Julian crept out and crossed a short distance, stopping in front of the tiny wall safe. As he watched, he knew that he had been there before. It was the place of hiding in the Palace under the Stars. Next he was hearing himself chant a tune. It was a strange sound, resembling what was backward speech. He remembered! It was the tune of the Keepers. Julian sang again.

Upon the utterance of each word there exploded a vast lighted ball out of nowhere. There came the sound of screams of terror and tumbling rock. Then:

"Julian, into the passage!"

The cavern was about to crumble. Then bang, everything was dark...Julian could no longer see anything in this recalling, but he continued to hear the voice or voices:

"Julian? Julian...JULIAN! Julian,...where are you!"

There was a moment of emptiness. Julian was now alone. He was not in the underground passageway. He felt the warmth of the Key in his grip and next out of the darkness came the sparkle of lights above and the torridness of what he recognized as a forest. Somehow he had been transported away and here to the forest. It was the Burning Forest.

*In the distance of his mind there was the
sense of an old voice. He was being drawn to
it.*

Just as Julian was thinking he understood, the
memory ended as unpredictably as it had started.
He was back in his shaft of light!

"This is so strange."

He had never physically left the shaft. The replayed memories were so real that he was led to
believe that he was actually moving from one
physical place to another. In fact, he was always
physically within his shaft, but spiritually, or intellectually, he was transported within the memory that was revealed. To the novice, it was impossible to discern any difference. Julian was
beginning to realized a difference, though it was
slow and uncertain. He was drifting between
thoughts and images. At times the imagery was
more real and distracting than his actual physicalness in this place. He felt phased. He was
questioning reality. He felt oozy and intoxicated
by the rapid switching within his mind and actual
experience within the journey of the shaft. He
could not quite explain the sensation, but it was
beginning to nauseate him. He found himself
wondering at the profundity of his emotional
being. It was so hard to relive the memories and

their impact. It had been hard enough the first time through, when he had originally been in them, at the time of their making. He raised his left hand to his face and wiped away the cool beads of sweat upon his upper lip. A thought struck him as he went through the motion.

"What if the first time hadn't been the original happening of the event?"

He began thinking of his father, and the long talks and stories he used to laboriously tell, always asking his son if he would swear to do his part when the time came. It seemed like he had had these exact thoughts before. He felt a déjà vu quandary envelop him:

"Was this an old happening or one yet to come. How many times before had this occurred? Or am I creating this experience as a result of the time and place I find myself?"

He had no option but to allow these thoughts of this 'past' event to continue. He wanted to revel in their nostalgia. Julian missed his father. He felt a wave of remorse overwhelm him. Had his father meant family responsibilities and the passing on of the craft, or something else? He remembered the numerous stories of ancient magic and the important mission to protect their Balance. He had realized that these were not just 'stories' during this flight from the *Evil*. Was he acting in the right way now? Was he fulfilling his destiny? Was he following the path that his father had prepared him for? Somehow Julian had always understood the truth that lay between the lines of the stories told by his father. Somehow he had always understood their greater meaning, but ignored this cognizance. As then, he did not now feel ready.

"Why hadn't I listened more to the words of the stories that were told to me in my youth? Why did I irritate and disappoint father so many times before... before it had been too late to make it up to him?"

His father must have known when the voice spoke during a future time of need, that it would then all be made more clear to his son. It would cause danger should Julian be too aware of details before there was a need. The father was protecting the son. If only Julian had had the chance to let his father see how he had matured from that young Jardian, into the person he was today. He desperately wanted his father to approve of him now!

These were old deeply hidden feelings. Julian was surprised and numbed by their resurgence. He recalled the tragic end to his father's life. It had been in the spring. It had been sudden and without warning. His father had been speaking with him before leaving in the early sunrise to supervise delivery of some stones to a new site:

"Julian, let's talk a bit."

"Oh not now. You'll be late, and I have to meet Sriol. We're going to hike to the sands."

"Just one moment. It won't take long."

"Faaather! I'll be late. Can't we talk this eve?" Julian was curt in his tone.

There was a pause. Then his father, as if he had realized something, said in a knowing soft way:

"Yes. Okay. We will talk later. Come here and hug me and then be off on your way."

Julian had hugged his father. He remembered a strange sensation as they had touched. A tingle went through him, as they had hugged. It was a different kind of parting than their usual morning departures. He broke from the embrace and said:

"Good-bye. See you later..."

See you later. How simple a phrase, as it rang out. He would never see his father again. There had been an accident. A large stone had broken loose from the cart and slid from atop crushing his father. It had been reluctantly accepted as just an unfortunate tragedy. But it was so unlike his father to have been so careless. Never before had his father stacked the stone upon his cart. Julian's mind lapsed. He could still see Lenore standing at the entrance of their home. She never said a word. There had been tears falling down her face as Julian had come running down the path to see her. Instantly he was aware of the loss. He ran toward her in disbelieve and an agony he had never before known:

"No. No. Not now!"

They fell into each others arms and wept.
Nothing more was said, as they touched the
depths of their despair.

What was unknown to both Julian and Lenore at this time, was the existence of the *Evil*. The *Evil* had discovered a drain in the Magic and tracked it to Jard. Julian's father had been unaware of this drain. In his stories and teachings he was transferring the ancient knowledge, and with them, small amounts of magic. Magic that would nestle within the son. Normally this type of drain would not have been detectable, but as all the other Chosen Ones no longer existed, even the smallest amount of trickle could be tracked. The *Evil* would eliminate this last

Chosen One!

Julian's father was caught unaware. Before the giant stone had fallen, he had seen the opaque cloud and heard a cursing from an ancient voice. It was too sudden for his ancient moles from within to act. Before he was crushed, he looked up and called out to his son:

"Boy! It is passed to you!"

Julian recalled how he had felt a quick jolt as he had been with his friends that day. He felt that something terrible had happened. He had cut his day short and hurried back to his home. He was being called!

"See you later," echoed again as he jumped back from the image and memory of that time. 'Later'... it had been such a long time. It had been long ago, and now felt closer. Julian could imagine that conversation as if it had just passed. He wished he had taken the time to talk with his father earlier in that sunrise. There was so much he would now say... time. How unpredictable... time—how elusive!

His mind turned away from the remorse of those events to one of consideration.

"What is time?"

It was a strange concern here in this place. He had no way of knowing or measuring its passage here. It was meaningless here. It was as if there was no time, just arbitrary memories, thoughts and emotions. Had he been here moments or weeks, or longer? He thought it was quite long. There was no way of knowing. All the memories he was having, were as if they were actually happening at the moment he originally experienced them. They were not just memories; they were real enactment's, and more. Though he was aware of his viewing, he was at the same time participating in the replayed scenes of memories. It seemed that this could go on without end, until there were no more memories, but maybe then there would be more memories of the experience of the memories?

If time was a measurement of passage, then all that was happening was surely measurable as Julian passed within this place. Though he had doubts as to his whereabouts, he could remember that he had once been elsewhere and not in this shaft. He held on to that realization. It brought him comfort. If there was nothing to measure here, then what of time? His mind was laboring to put his thoughts into sequence. They came in bits and pieces and did not flow smoothly together.

"Time. Maybe there is something of measurement. Perhaps it is not that there isn't time here, but rather it is a different type of time. A different way of regarding time and passage. A different set of rules. There are episodes here that occur, though not in any particular order, that cannot be linked in any way."

Julian was on the right road of understanding. Time here was more spatial. It did not rely or depend upon that which was before or after. In fact, there seemed to be no sensation of past or future. Everything remained as a present period. Things happened. There was no beginning or ending, just happenings. Things jumped from one to another. They remained active for random periods.

But what of himself? Was there a linkable connection of periods within his physicalness? Was he aging? Would he grow old and die here? If so, then there was time, in the sense that Julian understood. If not, then he wasn't really *here* in this shaft at all! His physicalness, he reasoned, demanded mortality. As he was not an immortal being, there must be time of the sort he was used to, here, otherwise there would be a tremendous anomaly and conflict within the Balance by his intrusion. If that were true, then he would not have been able to cross into this place. Surely there would be precautions that could prevent such crossings? There was no logical solution to his questioning.

Julian was tapping into his ancient awareness. He was doing it out of an ancient instinct. This type of knowledge was beyond a mere Jardian. The Old Ones knowledge was deeply placed within those chosen. Many differing levels, abilities and awarenesses, were locked away until times of need. At those times, only the smallest amount of awakening necessary was permitted to allow its host to overcome the particular danger that was presented at any particular time or place. This awakening would quickly fall back into dormancy once the danger was successfully passed. There would be a slight residual of a 'knowing', but precise details of understanding, would not be available. There would just be a sense of invincibility left within the host.

Julian was caught between what he was before this adventure began, and what he was now. The various levels of awakening that had happened, then the gradually becoming dormant again, his current level of awakening and the state of invincibility that residually had remained from previous awakening moles within him during other types of need, all were conflicting. So much had passed recently that Julian was still in a state of partial awakening between the many moles inside him and himself. The intricacy of what had been accomplished by the Old Ones within the Stoneman, and all Chosen Ones was complex. Truly the power of the Magic of the Balance was strong.

If this confusion was not enough, Julian's thoughts began to jump again. He helplessly wondered what memory would next be presented to his worn being:

He was watching from a side. The place was dimly lit with the color of glow plants. He felt as if he were in a cave. Off to the central area Julian could make out an oblong object that was pedestaled a length off the floor and emitting images that added a blue tone to the green of the glow plant. There were some forms which resembled the size and shape of beings grouped around the pedestaled glow. He surmised that the object was a screen of some sort. This was a strange place! He could not remember having ever seen such a sight. He suddenly was chilled. This was an Evil place. Inside, his guards were raising up. This was a home of Evil.

Julian watched the other beings that were

here. *They were ignoring him or were not aware of his presence. But he was still uncomfortable. He watched as one larger cloaked being lifted his hooded head up toward the direction of the others. One by one each of the others who were holding onto one another in order to form a circle of flesh released one another.*

"Do you believe he will accomplish the task?" one asked.

The larger cloaked being replied, "There has been much awakening in the past while. Things that we long ago thought were gone are still among us. Those that sent us here have placed much magic and planning in protecting the Balance of the Worlds. This was all unknown to us, and has been carefully worked out. Now that it is obviously triggered we will have to proceed cautiously. It will not be a simple task, but we are more prepared than most to deal with these handicaps. Those that are just awakening are not practiced in their magic. There is still time to take advantage of them in their naive period of discovery. It will be a matter of which group is quickest and shrewdest at applying these new found abilities."

"But what if they manage to enter the zone? What can we do then?" another questioned.

"We cannot allow that to happen. It will remove any influence we now have. We will be unable to predict the outcome if any other than ourselves discover the true purpose and Magic of the Key and Passwords of Promise. The others cannot return, but if the Magic is released prematurely, then there will be a mightier foe with which we must all deal."

There was a long silence. Nothing more was said. Then one by one each being left the tiny dim room except the large cloaked being. Julian felt a strange sensation and then without knowing how, he became the cloaked being. He began to feel the thoughts. He began to reminisce about Old Ones and a corporal life he had never known, yet he was participating in this being's thoughts. He was sharing the agonies. How he longed to be physical again. He missed the tactileness of existence. If only, he had not been discovered in his attempt to use the Passwords for his own gain! By now he would have learned much more about the Magic and risen to greater power. But he had been caught, along with his followers *and punished.*

An ancient anger against these punishers swelled within him. He must control it! Julian became terrified. He saw the depth of this being's memories. They were very ancient and powerful in the Magic, and Evil! In the first times of his banishment, he had almost gone crazy from the depravation of the senses. It was only due to his mastery and skill within the Magic, that he had been able to withstand the tremendous pressure that loss created. He also began to fixate on finding a way to reverse his condition. It had taken ages, but he found the way. There was an ancient Key that would unlock secrets of the Old Ones. The discovery of the Key was the final realization that all the time of searching for a missing link, which could provide him the necessary magic to return to the living, was now nearing fruition.

He moved closer to the screen. Julian began to understand that this jump had placed him in the hands of the Evil. This was the Evil that was following him. Chills ran down his spine. The cloaked figure leaned over and gazed into the screen. There was an old face coming into view. Then an angry voice:

"Impossible! How did you allow them to pass!"

"I gave them the knowledge."

"You W H A T ! They are beyond our control now. What will stop them from using the magic for their own gain? Each time we speak there are newer complications. I grow tired of the excuses."

"There has been other magic at work against me. Every occasion is matched or undermined by it. I cannot be expected to bring fast results when I must deal with the unpredictable. You have not warned me of the traps left behind! You of all others, should have known of these!"

"Yes. Those were not expected even by me. I thought that they no longer existed, or if they did, were too long in disuse to be of any threat. There are things that even I was not privy to in those times. Let us hope that is all of the tricks left by our predecessors"

The cloaked being didn't respond. The face faded into the void. Then for a moment there came a steady blue color across the screen. For the smallest amount of time the cloaked being looked into the screen. It caught a glimpse of something:

"WHO ARE YOU!"

Julian was discovered and instantly jarred out of the body of the being and away from this scene. As he left, he felt a touch of the powerful sting of the Evil. His body twisted in pain. Then he was back in the shaft.

The suddenness of the jumping out from the memory, and the turmoil within brought a tear to Julian's eye. He was silent. His thoughts were momentarily still. He was aware of his place inside the shaft. He saw its brightness. He sensed the vastness of the black void beyond. Other shafts flashed here, there and everywhere. The single teardrop slowly crept from the corner of his left eye along his lower eyelid to his cheek. It paused a moment then began flowing faster, being reinforced by more fluid from its source, down and dropping from his face. Julian made no cry. He remained stoic within this place.

"Please make this stop!" he cried in his head. His eyes were wide, red, and unblinking, as he stared through the shaft toward his uncertainty.

"Lenore. I am here with you. Call upon me and you will have all that you need. We have never been far apart. I am here, within you. I am here and will keep you out of harm from the *Evil*. I am sorry to have left you when I did. It was not my doing. It was because of this foul beast, the very one that threatens you even now. He will not have you as easily as he got me. Give your being over to the one in your dream. Trust in the Magic that you don't understand. It is deep inside you. It has always been there, lying dormant till a need arose. Now is that need. Now is the moment. Trust in your feelings. Act upon that sense. This

Evil is not what it appears. It is small, but together we are of the three. We have greater power within. Call upon it. Do not try or work too hard upon accessing its calling. Relax, and just be accepting of its existence. Do not believe. Do not doubt. Accept. It will release a great power. Do this now before it is too late. Your brother is in need. Help him now. Help him to help us all. Help him to save your sons. You hold the Magic. You are part of the Key."

This new voice was familiar to Lenore. She had not heard it since the earliest days of her youth. It was a voice she had missed and agonized over losing. Its leaving had created an emptiness that had proven throughout the time since, unfillable. Lenore learnt to adjust and to step around that void in her soul. There was no other way. Never did she expect to hear this voice again.

Everything else was so strange in her dream, but she knew this voice well, and it felt as comforting, strong, and loving as she remembered. It had always been the power which could calm and restore her. It would always rekindle the strength, purpose and possibility in her life. With its sound nourishing her whole being, there was nothing that she felt she could not accomplish. Her confidence soared. The memories of its timbre swelled Lenore's emotions. It was full of succor. Joy filled her aching heart.

"What can I do?" Lenore responded half nostalgically and half from the strain of these circumstances, with this phrase that she had used often in that early 'girl' period of her life in Jard. The times when the Stoneman's family had been whole. The times when a young Jardian female was eager to have all the grown up experiences, but couldn't wait; didn't want to go through all the tedious steps required. She would ask:

"What can I do? How can I do these things?" She had meant: how can I be doing the grown up things right away, without the drudgery of going through the steps. She was never very patient nor tolerant of the process. Though the circumstances were different here in her dream, the mood of the response was similar:

"Trust in the Magic. Accept your destiny. Do not rush," was said by the voice.

"But where have you been? What happened to you? Where were you? I needed you." Lenore appealed.

"Trust in the Magic. Accept your destiny." nothing more was said as the voice faded and repeated: "Trust in the Magic. Ac...ce...pt."

So many conflicting emotions and passions shot through Julian's being as he was carried on through the shaft. He was very worn. The tedium of this place in terms of his apparent inability to make sense or even control the events being presented to him, was frustrating. He was engulfed in a constant state of half thought. On the one hand he knew who he was: Julian the son of the Stoneman of Jard;

on the other he was someone else. This other self
came to him in glimpses without great substance.
It was mostly him... but more. There was slightly
more depth of personality. He suddenly recalled
a memory and as he realized that his mind was
about to once more 'jump' and replay it, sighed
a silent moan of dismay. Again he had no option
but to wait, watch and feel:

*Julian began to feel the metamorphosis. He
noted that the consciousness within was now
becoming more dominate over his mortal
being. His 'self' was watching while the
other consciousnesses directed. There was no
fear. The other beings were benevolent and
old. Their experience stretched as far back as
the original ones who had been first chosen.
As 'his' essence mingled, the depth of the
emotions and knowledge of them was as-
tounding, and beyond the ability to be expressed by normal words. He could sense far
back. It was a timeless experience. He was in
touch with many of his own from long ago.
He realized that though the consciousnesses
were being presented as though they were of
one linked strength, they were in reality an
ancient collection of all the individuals who
had also shared this common bond of being*

Keepers. If he so chose, Julian believed he could explore in an equal depth the entirety of the consciousnesses, any individual within him. All he had to do was focus on the one element he wished to know more about. Just as he was about to search for his father's consciousness, a voice spoke out:

"This is an old place to which we have returned." Darla's dominance spoke, "It is good to be alive and with friends!" The oldest communing was initiated.

"With friends," Julian answered.

Now Julian was in the Caverns near Tika. Before him stood Darla. She was so real. He reached with his arm to try to touch her. He then noticed that his nephews were also with him, but they were more. They were not the young Jardians that he had always known. 'Always' ran through his mind...always. There was a sudden awareness that they were also of the ancient consciousnesses. They were all connected somehow. But Darla seemed more powerful an image. He felt drawn to her, attached to her in some special way. He couldn't sense the reason why, but he knew that buried deep inside him he would find the answer. It was the security of knowing that he 'knew', that prevented him from seeking it out at this moment. He was entranced by her beauty. He could smell her softness. Her firm body. Her knowing smile. He fell captive to her sparkling blue eyes. He began to notice the little insignificant movements she made as she spoke and moved. He wanted to hold her. To feel her accepting within his powerful grasp. It had been so long! But now was not the moment for these thoughts or feelings. There were things of greater importance to be learnt. Still, the feelings lingered as the scene continued.

It was an unusual phenomenon. They were closer, and more intimate in their sense of one another, intuitively quick and determined. This was the Darla that Julian understood. He pulled back his arm and then became a participant:

"'D' give me Jewel so that we may finish what has been started." Julian affectionately spoke to Darla.

"A moment. It has been so long since I felt you around me. Come. Hold me once again. I have longed for your caress," Darla held out her arms. Julian moved and embraced his mate.

Such conflict. Now he was in her arms. Then from his nephews, who had disappeared and reappeared from this scene as quickly as Julian's thought jumped from one emotion and thought to another, came the comment:

"Don't you two ever stop!" Thiunn was embarrassed.

"It has been a long time." Eruinn silenced his brother to allow the distant loves to sparkle a moment in their union.

Then Julian's attention focused back upon Darla. The nephews disappeared from the image.

"We must continue," Julian held her as he spoke. The odd aspect of this to Julian as he watched and participated was that it was, and at the same moment wasn't him, Julian of Jard, who was speaking. It was another from within him. Another who had awakened and responded to Darla, causing her in turn to react.

Reluctantly releasing, Darla whispered, "I love you."

Julian felt a tinge so deep within that he was unable to speak. His eyes watered, and his heart gave a quick miss of a beat. He gazed into the beautiful eyes before him and, letting go, sobered his mind to the present. Darla gave him the sword as he withdrew.

"It has been long since our last reawakening. There is greater darkness this time. Let us hope Jewel can provide what we need." The other consciousness was now dominating. It was in absolute control. It knew exactly what to do. But not Julian. He felt left out. What was he to do? When this all had started, it was simple. Now everything was new and difficult. He felt a wave of depression approaching and did not wish to be absorbed by it.

At this change of thought, Julian jumped back. His awareness was back completely in the shaft. This time however, he was cognizant of something else. Somehow 'he' was controlling the jumping from memory to memory. He wasn't at the mercy of other powers as he had imagined. But he did not yet consciously comprehend the method of his control. Why was he not able to remember accurately much more about the names, places and events in his life as presented through the memories? Why could he remember some well and others not at all? Though these thoughts still nagged at him, he was overall beginning to settle from his astonishment of this place and his initial queries upon his arrival here. But how was he controlling? He thought of the river crossing. It had something to do with the Key. He felt a surge, and knew he was about to jump within his mind again. He braced himself:

"Julian. Julian. The time is near. You must listen carefully to what must now be heard."

The voice seemed to be coming from somewhere within the area. It was a voice, amongst many. The scene was blackness, though off in the distance was the hint of light.

"Father?" Julian was guessing. He couldn't comprehend. "Father is that you?"

"Listen. Do not speak now." An opaque image appeared in front of him. It wore the traditional garb of the Stonemason's of Jard. It was not his father. Julian did not question but awaited its words.

"You are not alone here. There are others who seek that which you are charged to protect. There is nothing that can be done to stop them. They have been given powerful knowledge from the Evil side of the Balance. You must go quickly. You can access the magic that you will need. You must not allow

the others to possess the Key. Use the powers
you have within. They must not prevail! It is
our, your, calling as a Stoneman's son. Do
what is necessitated."

"I don't understand all that has hap-
pened?"

"There is no time now. May the power of
the 'One' fill you!"

With that, the image, as before, faded.
There was nothing Julian could do. Or was
there? His mind turned to the shaft and in-
stantly he jumped.

He had not stopped to think on it before, but
now he began to analyze the occurrence of
jumping from image to image, emotion to emotion, thought to thought, within the replayed
memories. It was difficult. Everything was so un-
common, not only his surroundings, but also his
sense of being. He had many questions, but not
the luxury of pursuing any of them long because of the interference of the unpredictable
memory jumps. He was not even clear anymore
whether he was truly awake or asleep and
dreaming, or...perhaps he was dead! Perhaps he
had died from the fear of falling into the abyss,
and his body was being lifelessly tugged deeper
into the hold of the river below! In the panic of

this doubt, Julian needed some verification of his existence. He punched himself hard in his chest. It hurt. It felt very real. Or perhaps this was just another illusion. Perhaps Merm, having survived the fall from the Tunnel of Light, was now pulling his limp dead body to the riverbank in hopes of finding the Key. On thinking of the Key Julian's panic instantly evaporated.

"The Key...where was it?"

He searched in his mind for any trace of it. There, it was still in his grasp! He was not dead! He was not in the river, and Merm was nowhere near to him. This place must be real! He was still alive. But where was this place? Where was Merm and all the other dangers from which he was escaping? So many questions. With this new direction of his thought, he felt the surge of another memory jump. He continued to observe as his mind went to the scene:

Julian could feel the fear of the events leading up to his leap into certain death. He remembered as he witnessed in his mind the running approach of Merm from out of the blackness of the opening of the tunnel to the Cavern of Three and then the sudden running into, push and fall. It was an odd sensation. He was angry at the intrusion of this

Gott upon his own choosing and method of leaping into the canyon abyss. There was really no fear, just annoyance. He had been pushed out of the tunnel by Merm. As he fell toward the bottom of the abyss which would soon lead into the Pass river and what would be instant death, he had gripped harder onto the Key out of an instinct. His attention was on the Key and his thoughts turned to hope. Julian felt the strange lightness in his head and the rush of adrenaline throughout his body. He felt stimulated and alive as he turned and turned. He started to become dizzy, and without knowing why, he thrust his outstretched arms above his head. The action of his arms was to stabilize and stop his twisting as he flew. Merm was crying out after him, trying to claw his way through the length or so of the atmosphere that separated them both as they continued to fall. It was humorous to watch. For a moment it seemed like time was standing still, or maybe it was just the thrill of the free falling.

It seemed like an eternity had passed. Julian, still grasping the Key, considered his next steps—next steps! Why had he thought this? Was there a way out? Could he survive

this? Many flashes went through his mind. As
long as he held the Key and focused upon
the 'singular thought of hope' he would be
rescued from an otherwise terrible fate. As he
fell, he understood more and seemed to be
becoming more, but he didn't know what. He
felt different. More than just a Stoneman's
son from Jard.

This memory was a repeat! It was an earlier replay. One of the first memory jumps in his
thoughts since arriving in the shaft, amongst this
blackness. This was the first pattern or sequence
of events he had discovered here. By repeating,
Julian determined that there was a pattern occurring. The experiences being presented here were
not just an assortment of randomly chosen items,
though he could not identify the pattern. As he
realized this, his mind had jumped back into the
shaft. He *was* affecting the memory jumping.

After a contemplative pause, Julian tried to
think, or feel something that would prompt a
jump. He wanted to test to see if his hypothesis
was correct: that he was somehow influencing his
experiences here. He had noticed that whenever
a jump occurred, just before it, he had felt an
emotion, or had a thought upon the subject that
thereafter materialized and played. Julian con-

centrated. While tightly closing his eyes, he strained and tensed his abdominal muscles, but he was left unchanged and still in the shaft. He could not understand. What was different about his trying to *force* a jump, as opposed to a casual thought or emotion that prompted or acted as catalyst to a jump?

"There must be something more. Some aspect of the experience that I have missed."

He felt more tired and frustrated. Just as he thought he might be making some progress toward gaining some control, or understanding of himself and his environment, he was thrown back into its subjugation.

The disorientation of this place was once more overpowering him. He turned his attention away from his mind and onto his physical situation. The void was still black, and the shaft the only source of illumination. It was a multicolored glowing with the hint of a green hue. All about him was the glow. There was nothing else here with him inside this circular beam. He was not standing, nor sitting. There was no weight pressuring any part of his body. He was floating steadily in place; being suspended within the shaft by a type of energy. He wondered at its source, "Am I a prisoner here or a passenger?"

His mind had been so preoccupied by the jumping from memory to memory, that he hadn't had time to examine his physicality in this place. He decided to attempt this now. The obvious place to begin was to do a check of his physical well being. He moved the various extremities of his body: arms, legs, one by one; he gave a shaking to his head. All were in order. He then shook his hands, and while doing so, thought about moving his whole person to his left. To his amazement his body position moved into that direction. He may not be able to control the psychological, but the physical was a different story. He was pleased with this discovery. Gradually he learned that he could shift his position within this energy by a slight shifting of either of his hands and a corresponding thought along with it. To move toward his left he would out turn his left hand and think LEFT. Immediately his whole body would move toward the left of the shaft. Up, down, right, turn around, flip over, under: all these were controlled by the various movements of his hands and thoughts. No other motion of his body seemed to affect his positioning, and his hands only changed his direction within his traveling forward, when there was the corresponding thought in his mind to do so. If he shifted his hand without the thought of changing his direction, then there would be no such change to his positioning within the shaft.

It was entertaining. He did not yet appreciate the similar ability of control within his 'mind memory jumping'. He was too afraid to allow his mind to think on anything but this new discovery of motion. He did not wish to risk any more jumps than necessary. He had realized that as long as his thoughts were focused he had fewer jumps. If his mind wandered, then he would be somehow bombarded with a multitude of jumps. He was pleased with this knowledge, though he wasn't certain of its source. He did realize that it was an old wisdom and it was a part of him, but did not analyze the reason, he needed time to collect himself. The distraction of the motion was perfectly timed. The jumping for now had stopped. If it was due to his own abilities he was pleased. He would not question how he accomplished this feat. If it was not due to his own controlling, then he would like to get as much stability as he could till the next jumping. Perhaps he would learn something that could help him here. He continued his physical maneuverings.

After mastering his movement within the shaft,

he began to pay attention to other observations. He was feeling slightly more calm than his first few moments here in the shaft. Nothing in this place followed any discernible sequence or pattern. The only exception to this had been this last jumping. But now he wasn't sure if that was true either. Every occurrence was random and came out of any direction. It was affecting him. He found it increasingly more difficult to think in any organized manner or rely upon what he saw or thought. Images appeared and disappeared in his mind without any logical connection. There were no links between the type or quantity of thought. He was losing track of any normal type of awareness, and this was causing him some discomfort. He found himself expressing images to himself and experiencing their visualized meaning as opposed to symbolic words. He had been jumping from image to image and their rate of passage was increasing. He was not able to keep up with them and then along came this reprieve. He wasn't certain why, or how long this pause in the mental jumping would last. But he felt he had something to do with its occurrence. His thoughts kept moving from absolute clarity of purpose and knowing, to complete confusion and distrust of everything he experienced. The repetitiveness of all this was annoying.

He continued to struggle to learn, and acquire some sense or order. Something inside him slowly was awakening.

"I must stop trying to place this world of the shaft and void within the confines of Jardian world view. I must look for a different connecting thread." he spoke to himself.

Straightness of thought was not applicable, it would only confound. Linear experience and thought were not possible. In order to comprehend all that was passing, Julian had been trying to find a meaning and a placement within linear time.

"Where is a beginning, middle and end?"

He wanted to place things in a sequence. A sequence that would give a concreteness to his own reality. A uniformity of thought and deed. In his attempts to continue thinking this way here, he had become frustrated and frazzled. He would have to stop pressuring to force another world's order and meaning into this place.

In this non linear world, he had not fully appreciated that his random thoughts were being actualized. Any thought could be explored by merely directing the slightest bit of energy into its direction. In the other world from which Julian came, these multitudes of random thoughts were filtered by way of his physical abilities of speech and communication. Many of those thoughts concurrently held, would not be expressed or examined. This, in a linear world such as Jard, gave the meaning of that existence. It would be impossible to accept, understand and communicate every thought within and behind a thought of every aspect of a Jardian thinking brain, and have any sense of meaning or sequence. There would be far too many tangential ideas to deal with. Somehow the thoughts within those of the worlds like Jard, had to be sifted and included or excluded according to their contribution to the continuing of the actual direction of the expressed idea of the moment. It was both very limiting and at the same time crucial for any growth toward learning of the Magic and moving along the tiers, for those inhabitants of those worlds. It was the natural way.

The Old Ones had overcome these types of thought siftings or limits, and discovered more complex and complete understandings of invincibility. Their level of ability took a long time to nurture, and would not be applicable to those of the worlds of Jard. As a result, only the sifted expressed thoughts of those of these worlds were given communicative priority. Given the right amount of time, Jardians and others like them, would grow to be gradually capable of more complexity in their 'expressive' knowledge. Here, in this place, on the other hand, all thoughts could be seen, heard and experienced at once or separate or together. Here, was not controlled by physical limits, or means of verbal communication. It was a place of thought. The power of thought. The Magic of the mind. Here required a greater mental control and ability than Jard.

The lack of any sequential ordering for any of these thoughts was an additional dilemma beyond the sensorial uniqueness of the shaft, for anyone not prepared for this place. It turned everything inside out. This was a place of non linear progression. Julian would find no beginnings, middles, or endings, because there were none here. These concepts did not exist.

Julian gripped harder onto the Key. He still needed a tangible object to remind him of his 'being'. The touch of the Key made him a little more reassured. This place was affecting: his mind, his sense of being and thought. The touch of the Key began to make him feel slightly more in control.

"Who are YOU?"

Julian had jumped back to the last part of the previous haunting jump. The cloaked figure in this screen room was the Evil. It was Dorluc. But Julian having never met him was not aware of his name, just that this was Evil and after him.

"Who are YOU?!" came a raspy and old threat. "Wri noon fvra bi noik. Hoiu dsa rew bu hgaas! Lyr ziog ved xsoq ki jhec. Ici Ni Ban yi!"

It was a strange language. Julian could only recognize that last sentence. These were words spoken before. He was not able to translate the meaning, but he knew the sense of what it meant. These were old words. Magical phrases to overpower and harm him. Without thinking Julian counter-manded:

"Ho ti rec gho! Ici Ni Ban YI! Gnui bek moo!"

Suddenly Dorluc raised his head, throwing back his head in the motion and causing his hood to reveal his face. Julian gasped. It was terribly old and deathly white. The wrinkles hung and dragged the visage heav-

ily down. The eyes were red and penetrating.
Julian was spellbound:

"So you are the thief! You have found
sanctuary in the Labyrinths. But not for
long. Not for long. Not for long. Hri nuuk
tre."

With that a chill of fear entered Julian. This
Evil had found him. It would not be long
before he was here with him. He must es-
cape!

He jumped. He was back in the shaft trembling
and weak.

In the ever mounting disorientation that was
being presented to him through this place, he
began to comprehend that all that was happening
to him, was designed to distract. Though he was
shaken by this last scene, he noted that whenever
he felt about to lose his mind and had simplified
or narrowed his thoughts to one idea, then he
managed to regain some security and mental
composure, and escaped the scenes. In order to
survive, he determined that he must realign his
attention to only those basic ideas that were of
priority to his present condition: *he must secure*
the Key from the Evil and allow nothing else to
stand in the way. He tried to fill his mind with
that concept. Almost immediately he began to

sense more calm within. It was a relief to the now very exhausted Julian. He flattened out both of his hands indicating a recline motion, and his body position moved to one of relax. He lay still, eyes opened wide as he stared into the blackness that lay just past his shaft of light. He kept all thought aimed at his purpose, while marveling at this place. He dared not allow his thoughts to stray. He required some rest from all of this mayhem. He felt that wherever he was now, it was better than where he had just come, away from both the *Evil* and Merm. By now, in that other world, he was certain he would have drowned and be dead in the water.

Julian was in the transition zone between the world of Jard and that of Magic, though he was not fully knowledgeable of this fact, place or route. This void was the buffer zone between the two places. It allowed the separate existence of vastly differing and opposing universes. It provided a means of linking each, while at the same time keeping each isolated. Travel between them was possible by way of the shaft, for those knowledgeable such as the Old Ones. It connected not only worlds, but also times, past, present and future.

There were many of these zones and shafts of

light, or as they had been named by the Old Ones: these Labyrinths of Light. They were a natural phenomenon which had revealed themselves to the Old Ones after many generations of study and growth in their Magic. Through these pathways, the Old Ones had gone on to their next level. These passages were not intended for the undisciplined novice. They were intended for use only by those of greatest level within the Magic. Though the shafts were meant for one direction of travel, they could be used other ways. Once in the Labyrinths a noticeable drain to the Balance occurred and would be felt by all of the Chosen; a drain that would alert all including the Old Ones.

Unauthorized or unprepared entry would lead to the total destruction of the mind of such a user. One exception had been allowed: those charged with the protection of the Key and *Passwords of Promise*. This was not out of malice, but rather the nature of the Labyrinths. They presented such an opposing conceptualization of reality that any who entered required enormous abilities of magic to withstand the multitude of conflicting ideas that were to be unveiled upon any journey amidst them.

The energy that fed these Labyrinths was directly connected to the Magic in its most pure form. The strongest power of Magic was accessible to those who entered and were able to use it. Julian had accessed it by using the Key along with his power of thought as a Stoneman and Keeper. Like all of those before him, he, during time of need, could enter. He had unwittingly initiated the process by which he could be transformed out of his dangers and into a place of safety and well being.

It was not only through the Key and his inherited skills that he had managed to escape Merm and his fall, but also by focusing on his obligation as a Keeper of the Key to journey till the hiding place was found. There had been an intervention on his behalf by all of those before and within, whose consciousnesses were now awakened in Julian to their full capacity and no longer passively dormant.

Long ago, when the first Stoneman had been entrusted with the obligation of protecting the instruments of the Magic and the Balance, there had also been given special access to areas of the Magic unavailable to any others of their Worlds unless they were of the greatest Magic. The Old Ones, once knowledgeable of these mysteries, had provided such access in order to give advantages to those who might be threatened by other *Evil* powers. These Labyrinths were a place of refuge given during moments of extreme duress, or as a means of passage beyond. Through it a Keeper could be transported away from the dangers that followed and be given another opportunity to accomplish his task. The fact that Julian now found himself in this place, demonstrated that the level of his jeopardy had been of the utmost height! Here in this place, once his purpose could be clearly communicated by his singleness of thought, he could rest and have his strength rejuvenated.

There were many such places as these which could be intuitively accessed by a Keeper, but only at the time of need were they made available. He was not yet permitted to pass beyond the void. He must return and complete his calling. Two times earlier, similar places and powers had been given in order to allow Julian to complete his mission. A mission that had almost been finished until Merm had appeared and pursued Julian into the Cavern of Three. Not only was it important to hide the Key, but also, it would help Julian gain access to levels of Magic otherwise unattainable. The Key allowed the user to gain entry to these places of power, these places, these

Labyrinths of Light. Here the user could learn more of the Magic of the *Passwords*. A magic that could ward off the *Evil* powers of the Worlds.

To the beginning entrant there was a period of transition in acclimatizing oneself to the differences of this place. Traps or tricks were played upon the minds of those entering. Traps and tricks that only those of the Old Ones could survive. Part of Julian's disorientation was a result of these traps and tricks. As those of the Old Ones would be in the Labyrinths, out of selfless acts, they were most easily protected from the dangers of the Magic of the Labyrinths. The strength of focus on the pureness of one selfless thought, the protection of the Key, had temporarily prevented harm from befalling Julian. It was through this focus that he would benefit and be better prepared to carry on his duty. It was most complicated. But it worked. Only Julian had crossed into the Labyrinths. Dorluc was unable to enter the Labyrinths because of his banishment. Merm did not have the knowledge or instruments of power that might have allowed him entry. Also Wakan could not chance discovery by the Old Ones of his alliance with the power of the *Evil* side of the Balance. He would be quickly overpowered and dealt with. Julian was safe for the moment, but in the Land of No Form two were planning:

"He has passed. We may not follow. There is nothing to be done while he is in the Labyrinths." Wakan was pensive.

"Will the others be alerted by his entry?" Dorluc questioned.

"Yes, but they will not link the cause to us. They will know of the link to the Evil but it will be connected to the Gott and its source therefore a mystery. They will begin to search."

"His magic will soon be strong."

"Yes, but no match for our combined strength. We will soon have the final confrontation. You must gather all your allies. Cause diversions in the three Worlds. This will upset the Balance and hide awareness of us from the others. It will not be long now. Soon it will begin!"

"It will be done."

So many conflicting stimuli were still growing within Julian. He had no way of measuring their length of duration. He had lost track of how long he had been here. He believed he had just arrived, but perhaps it was much longer. There was no longer a sense of entry or exit points. He simply existed in a place whose only apparent linear or measurable movement was the shaft. He felt as if his mind would explode under this pressure. Julian was overcoming the traps through the passage. He had managed to avoid the destructive power of the initial disorientation. He was growing tired, and between his mood swings of safety to panic, was becoming lost. He was loosing track of himself.

Outside of his body there were no noises. This reminded him of his previous submersion in the river and another aspect of that experience—the voice! It was all so confusing and muddled. No thoughts followed any particular order or path. In fact, they all popped in and out of his mind, in and out of context. It was enough to drive one mad!

Because the muddle in Julian's head was completely distracting, he had not noticed that the shaft was now changing; that the sights surrounding him were becoming more constant and less arbitrary; that he was, indeed, affecting the change. But this did not concern him now. His attention was trying to find a calm ground away from this abstract, obtuse place. He again focused upon his purpose: he must secure the

Key from the *Evil* and allow nothing else to stand in his way. He concentrated on this thought amongst the disorder that was being presented to him visually, and sensorially. He was alive and felt he knew he was acting correctly. The strain was immense.

Just at the moment when he experienced a minimal control, another distraction was faintly audible. This time, unlike the visual input, it was of an audible nature. It was a sound! A very faint and delicate sound. He could hear a noise. He now trusted that he had heard something in this silent place. He strained to identify its source.

"Why is it familiar? Where had I heard this before?—It is the voice of the river! Yes, it had the same tone and texture."

It was beginning to speak, but was not quite clear. Julian could hear the whisper tone. He definitely could make out the sound of words being spoken, but not what the words were. He was still being distracted by all of the other influences here in this place. He became desperate.

"What is the voice?"

He needed to hear the voice! He placed his palms over his ears and maintaining his grip upon the Key, tried in a useless effort to hear better. But there were no other external sounds to block. It was internal. In yet another effort to find peace he pushed his mind to his singular purpose: he must secure the Key from the *Evil* and allow nothing else to get in his way. He closed his eyes from the distraction of the Labyrinths of Light, and repeated over and over in his thoughts his purpose:

"I must secure the Key from the *Evil* and al'ow nothing else to get in the way...must secure the Key from the *Evil* and allow nothing else to get in the way...must secure the Key from the *Evil* and allow nothing else to get in the way."

The more he went over this thought the clearer the voice became. The voice was repeating one word. Yes, it was only one word! It was coming closer, as if it was issuing from a great distance. It approached in waves. Closer and louder, till finally with a sudden impact:

"JULIAN."

4

"What a fool to jump!" M e r m muttered reproachingly.

But he hadn't. Merm had been running out from the Cavern of Three and into the lighted tunnel. His intention was to catch up with the thief and apprehend him before both the Key and the thief could get away. Merm was so close to the Southlander as he approached through the Tunnel, that he did not care to take the chance of losing this second opportunity of regaining the Key and all the power that he could wield from it. He was running with all his might, and was short of breath, his chest still heaving from the exertion of the fight within the Cavern, and this pursuit. He had abruptly ended the engagement with the other Southlanders, taking no time to rest, and continued after the one with the Key. He had not yet realized that everything he was doing, was being influenced by something, or someone else. All he remembered was that he had noticed the exiting of the one Southlander only after it had been drawn to his attention by an inner voice. He believed it was the voice of the image of his dreams, but in all the furor was not sure of this assumption.

These dreams had always been with him, since his rise to power over the Gottland, and more recently on this journey to Tika. He trusted them. There had been many strange awakenings on this trip. He was still pondering over the chain of events that had led up to his 'leaping' into the abyss after the thief and into a certain death as he ran through the Tunnel. What had overcome him? Why had he been so reckless in his actions? It was unlike him to act so impetuously. He always had made it a habit to place another ahead of him in any situation where there was risk. If there were no other available, then he would postpone his actions where possible, or proceed with tremendous care. He had done neither on this occasion. He turned back that last few measures of his life as if they were part of a musical score, that he might examine more closely and replay without mistake, or in a different manner. He was examining every aspect of this 'composition' for the precise movement that had led him upon the sequence of events from the path through the tunnel after the Key and then, on to act so quickly and rashly by leaping into this abyss. He could not accept his stupidity in taking such an action. He searched his memory. He needed to understand, if it was the last thing he did. Why had he not shown more caution at the opening to the abyss? What had come over him to cause him to act in such a way? At what point did he let go of his regard for his own safety, and why? He searched his memory, quickly examining the past moments leading to this fate. He pushed his thoughts back and recalled from the beginning.

It was in the Cavern and he, with the Rider, were in combat with the Southlanders. He marveled at how his use of his illusionary magic had become stronger. This improvement had not been noticed during the adrenaline rush of the fighting. He assumed that it was a result of the stress of the fight, but the greater power was in fact more than the emotional rush of the conflict. He was being assisted by another. He felt stronger, as if another had stepped into his soul. His ability to use this magic was increased, and with his new strength, suddenly he felt the winning advantage. Along with this new strength he began to feel a compulsion. A compulsion that had always been there unnoticed by his conscious mind until recently, since he had found the Key in Norkleau! All of this was, unbeknownst to Merm, connected to the influencing image in his dreams, and the voice that he was now hearing. He trusted this voice which he believed was the same as his dreams. He accepted it. He no longer cared if he was in control of himself, or this voice. He wanted the Key at any cost! This was so unlike him. He felt that this strange force within him had been the same one that had helped him to his position of power. He told himself that he must listen and allow himself to be its vehicle. It was telling him to go:

"I must stop the one with the Key! I must not let

the Key go! This is the moment. Take advantage of this moment! There it is!"

Merm had found the point in the sequence. This was the movement. It had set in motion the playing out of the orchestration that had led him here—here to his doom. It had been summoned from within himself. Out of nowhere it had suddenly materialized as he fought with the Southlanders in the Cavern. It was the same *Evil* image that had confronted Thiunn in Julian's cottage at Jard. Merm thought it had been his magic, but it was otherwise. It was the greater *Evil*! It drew Merm's eye to catch a fleeting glimpse of the thief with the Key escaping into the lighted tunnel. From inside the voice demanded:

"Go after him. Get the Key!"

There was no questioning or thought of choice. He turned toward, and ran after Julian and on to his death.

But he *had not* leaped from the Tunnel into the abyss. Merm recalled the moments. He could see in his mind's eye the thief hurrying up the lighted tunnel, panicked and looking back over his left shoulder to see who followed after. Merm saw the fear in the face of the thief; the desperation of his running out of any more choices. The thief was becoming a victim of his own destiny, but still did not accept the inevitability of it all. Beyond the thief, a few more lengths, there was a large bright circular glow. The tunnel abruptly ended. The thief arrived and stopped at what was obviously its edge. Merm quickly understood. It was a dead end. There was nowhere to go. Merm, from his experience through all of the campaigns he had fought during his long career in the Gott military, recognized a drawn taught look on the thief. It was the same lost desperate look that all prey or defeated acquired at that moment just before the kill or defeat. The moment between hysteria and desperation. The decision to 'fight or flight', where both seemed to offer the same result. It was now merely a choice between the lesser of two certain deaths.

Merm had been so absorbed by the chase and the excitement it afforded him, that he had neglected to acknowledge the proximity and influence of the force that compelled him. There was a frenzy within.

"The Key must not cross! Go after him. Get the Key!"

Merm was being directed by this power. The combination of Merm's emotional elation and the control of the power caused a confusion, resulting in a delay of signals. When Merm reached the end of the tunnel, his physical being said stop—beware, while the non physical power that was controlling him, forgetting the limitations of the flesh said:

"Go on."

The consequence was that Merm was not able to comprehend in time the rapid need to adjust his pace and stop, before falling over the Tunnel's edge into the abyss. It had not been clear that the thief would jump, and he hadn't; neither had Merm. The thief, resentful of this large smelly Gott's intrusion, had been pushed over by the momentum of Merm's confused actions. Both were caught by the finality of another's choice. Both were falling into the abyss. They had not jumped of their own accord.

Merm understood. The loud reverberating wail of the rushing air as it was forced through his unkempt facial hair and over his clothes causing them to flap and snap, beating any of his exposed skin, began distracting him. He was falling. There was nothing he could do, and knowing what was behind the events that had brought him to and over the Tunnel's edge brought little comfort.

Merm was twisted in every direction as he fell.

He dreaded what was to be the outcome. He tumbled more with each movement he made of his limbs. Over and over he spiraled. As he was contorted by the fall through the emptiness of the atmosphere, he strained back his head to try and see the thief. He wanted to keep an eye on him as they both fell. There was still the thought in Merm's opportunistic mind, of the smallest hope that he might survive the fall. In that case he would quickly grab hold of the Key from the Southlander after they had fallen into the watery depths of the mighty river below. That would only be possible if he saw where the Southlander entered the river and was able to catch him in the rush of the river's flow. If only he could get closer, before the final impact.

"If only I could reach the bearer of the Key before we reach the river. Then I can hold him and drag him to the river's edge and get the Key. If this thief survived the fall he would surely not survive my hold."

Merm was planning. He and the Southlander were both very close to one another as they fell. There was no more than an arm's length separating them. Merm could see that the thief was struggling to find some sort of stability and ground-like orientation. They were both in tandem to each other in the canyon abyss. Merm could smell the fear of the other. It was not only caused by the anxiety of the fall, but also the dread of being finally caught, alive or dead. Sensing this made the huge filthy Merm try to get closer, and within reach. Merm was clawing at the air as they both continued their free fall. He was dizzy and very disoriented. It seemed as if he was closing the gap. He doubled his efforts at this stratospheric swim.

Both tumbled. It was clear to Merm that he would soon be able to take hold of Julian. The thought of death awaiting below disappeared from Merm's concern. There was a confidence replacing it. He could overcome the apparent fate of the fall. He 'knew' that this was not to be his demise. He was not going to die. It was not wishful thinking. He just knew that this was not to be his destiny. He did not yet know how he could survive this foolhardy leap into the abyss, but he 'knew' from within, that he would!

After Merm had taken the initial step over the Tunnel's edge, Dorluc was alerted. It was as if an alarm had been set off. If Merm was harmed in any way, then the Key would be lost. Too much effort and purpose had been devoted to this one Gott. Dorluc had learnt to take precautions due to a previous disaster—the last minute loss of the Key by the Lord Ho. Ho had been corrupted by the power of the Key and not carefully overseen by the *Evil*. Had he been under closer scrutiny, Ho could have been swayed from the corruption, that once released, was impossible for Dorluc to undo. In the end, Ho's greedily calling upon the magic held by the Key had overwhelmed and destroyed him. The *Evil* suffered a terrible set back. Just when there was no hope of ever connecting, and influencing another of the physical worlds, along had come Merm.

Merm had been a strapping young Gott Trooper interested in more than mere soldiery. He held ambitions, lofty goals. He was much more intuitive in his awareness, and was well versed in all Gott custom and lore. During his earliest years he had been shunned by his peers. At that time, Merm was considered mediocre for a Gott in size and demeanor. So, he was left out of most of the activities of youth. He turned to learning, to pass his time and feel less lonely. Books became his closest companions. This brought more ridicule from his young peers, but by then he was far too engrossed in the mysteries of the oldest of Gott writings, the Forbidden Books.

There was not much in the way of good record keeping or writing by the Gotts, both being viewed as undignified, but the writings that did exist were thoroughly scribed. Merm studied and excelled. It did not take long for this ill proportioned insipid, but promising young Gott to be noticed by one of the few chroniclers, for that is what the Gott named those who kept to words more than fighting. Merm was encouraged to learn the craft of the chronicler, and was given more and more opportunity to read and learn the ancient Gott writings. As time progressed, Merm displayed a great talent for the ancient language, and soon became expert in the interpretation of those hieroglyphics. Where he had lacked in physical prowess, he excelled in his absorption and command of the Gott history, lore, and hints of the powerful knowledge available to those of highest position in the community. He was not aware that the incredible knowledge acquired by his deciphering and reading of the various old writings, was unlocking and tapping into an equally incredible old power. Merm saw an opportunity to advance and 'show' all those who had scoffed at him, how foolhardy they were. He would know more. He would get even!

It was about this time that Dorluc had sensed an

inquiring new mind within the Magic. A mind that could be receptive to his influencing. This was another chance to complete what Ho had failed to do. It did not take long for Dorluc to track the source as being Merm, and to begin the process of influencing through the dream state.

In his secret lust for power and knowledge, it was made clear to Merm that he needed total access to all the writings of the Gott. Only then could he be respected. In order to do this he would have to acquire much more stature and power. Dorluc found it easy to act as a catalyst, stimulating the submerged emotions of: insecurity, inadequacy revenge, and greed, that were contained in this particular Gott.

Gotts generally were stupid in matters of intellect. Though this one showed little sign of difference, he was much more shrewd. This one had greater intellectual prowess. But this would not be enough to be of help to Dorluc. Mere mental ability did not offer much in terms of real physical power. Merm needed to be in command of more. Merm needed to gain and raise in political strength. He needed to be in leadership in order to be of use to Dorluc's cause. Dorluc would maneuver Merm into achieving both their ends. There was the need for Merm to gain experience and respect within the main military forces of Gott society. Dorluc awaited the proper opportunity to commence this process. When Merm had reached the appropriate age, he was required being a Gott, to do military service. All Gotts of both sexes were called. Here was the occasion that Dorluc could use. Though Merm was not happy about this forced duty, he would in the end, with Dorluc's aid, look back on this as one of the most profitable experiences of his life.

It did not take long for success in his military career. It seemed that the insipid youngster was transformed through the rugged training, into a well proportioned, if not larger, specimen of a Gott. By the end of his training he graduated with Sub Field rank, and so impressed his superiors with his knowledge, military astuteness and temperament, that he was immediately given a small field command. This was almost unheard of. Only Lord Ho had been so capable and honored in the recent past. This of course, drew even more attention to an already rising star.

Merm, through Dorluc, had developed the strength of surrounding himself with capable subordinates. Submissive Gotts who realized that they, through Merm, could gain much wealth and influence. Rmont was one of the shrewdest of these subordinates. It was a fortuitous marriage for all, including Dorluc. Not only would Merm be manipulated by Dorluc through the dream state, but also he would be diplomatically positioned by Rmont in the real worlds to reach the requisite heights of power. He would then be allowed access to all the secrets of the Forbidden Books, which only those in leadership were given. This would be necessary in order to locate the powerful tool of the Magic. A locating process that Dorluc was not able nor permitted to initialize. Merm must accomplish that on his own, or as it turned out, with the help of Rmont.

Campaign after campaign. Success after success. Dorluc's altering of any opponents disapproving energies. All these things eventually catapulted Merm into the Gott political court. Merm had developed a great talent for leadership. Rmont also recognized that this, if channeled correctly would, after Rmont's smoothing away of any rough offending edges, place Merm as the Lord of the Gotts with himself powerful in the background. Everything was proceeding better than any of the three could have ever expected. Each in their separate places became more cautious and protective of their accomplishments. Except Merm who, convinced of his own invincibility, similar to the way Ho became changed ages ago, became more arrogant. It was not yet as pronounced as Ho, but it did raise concern between the others that it affected.

So had begun the interdependence between Merm, Rmont, and surreptitiously, Dorluc. To this point all had gone so rapidly well. After Merm had been proclaimed Lord of The Gott, he was then able to satisfy the lusting after the secrets of the Forbidden Books. Merm began the searching of any and all allusions, no matter how small or obscure, relating to the Key. At first Merm thought that the references to the Key were just myths, but he was intrigued by the consistency with which it was mentioned, and the strange manner in which the words relating to it were quietly placed within the page. It was finally in the Fifth Book of Ho, of the Forbidden Books, that Merm stumbled across the mention of a Magical Key, and that it would give to the beholder the greatest of power and Magic.

"That's odd," he pondered. "Why would something so important be so underscored? There must be more about this Key."

After the initial discovery was made, Merm did not realize that it was Dorluc who had implanted the curiosity to continue to search for more information on the Key. Eventually Merm had pieced together enough of the scattered references to understand that the Key had existed and still did exist. Further, he concluded that all that was said of its powerful magic was probably true. Why else try to conceal its existence by the multitude of scant references. There were too many references of the Key to ignore. There was even mention of the place where it was hidden, but Merm was having difficulty in precisely translating the language of the chroniclers who had written these accounts. They were so scattered and remotely placed by a great number of different chroniclers over a lengthy time period, that the subtleties of meaning were almost impossible to determine within complete reliability. He did manage to translate that the Key lay hidden somewhere in the Northlands. It did not indicate why it was hidden or by whom, just that it was protected and that there were three warnings or conditions to heed. Merm wasn't sure of the exact interpretation of the meaning of these phrases. He was more intrigued with locating the hiding place.

Rmont had been of great assistance to Merm during this time. Merm had been so obsessed with the search, both in the Forbidden Books and the digging that commenced, that he had essentially taken over the day to day running of the Gottland. Merm trusted Rmont as long as it suited his need. It was during this time, through Rmont's keen hands, that the Gotts began to organize and run themselves more efficiently. It was an authoritarian state, the looseness that had found its way into the Gott after the Separation War was eliminated. Profit and accountability of every part of the military machine was fine tuned. There was a renewed pride in being Gott; a sense of the strength of the times under Ho. A wave of might was swelling forth. The desire to dominate the Worlds and break free of the Separation War Treaty limitations became a fervent thought in the minds of all Gotts. Rmont rode with the wave and Merm was pleased as long as those under his rule were content. The Gotts anticipated that great things were about to happen, that the Great Lord would re-establish the Empire of the pre Treaty times. That is why no questions were asked, after Merm decided to start the search at the sites where he had narrowed the hiding place of the Key to be. Each Trooper was willing and dedicated to his Lord. When it became clear that more help would be needed to quicken the search, slave labor was instituted. A system of competition and Reward developed. This was great sport! The Gott were not sure of the motives of the Lord with his frantic digging, but many felt it was just a ploy to unite and strengthen the Troops under a cause in preparation for the invasion to dominate the outside Worlds. There was much speculation. Only Rmont and Merm knew the real reasons. Regardless of the reason, Rmont was pleased to witness the surge in morale. Rmont was also proud.

All these events had contributed to arriving at this moment. As Merm fell into the abyss, everything seemed such a waste.

"Surely this could not be the end!" he thought as he struggled through the air. He would not give up. "If only Rmont were here to help. I will miss him. The fool."

Merm was saddened to have lost Rmont in the Cavern. He still had need of him. "If only he had not been lost till after the reclaiming of the Key!"

Merm's thoughts grew angry with his frustration. He stretched his head around again to find the Southlander who now was just a quarter of a length away. He needed some help. As a last resort, Merm's mind called to the power of the image that had appeared in his dreams. The being who had identified itself and offered help with the magic of the illusions. Merm hoped there would be an answer and rescue.

Since Dorluc had last appeared to Merm through the dream state in the Burning Forest, before the crossing into the zone of the Old Ones, he had made certain to keep part of his consciousness linked to the Gott Lord. This was done more out of a curiosity than any other need. Dorluc had believed that it was to be merely a matter of when, not if Merm would recover the Key from this Jardian. Though Dorluc was banished from his ancient home of Tika and forbidden to enter its zone, the expulsion had not included his non physical wanderings. At the time of banishment to The Land of No Form, it was never contemplated by the Old Ones that Dorluc would ever be able to discover how to interfere from there, to the physical world, as a formless being. At the time of his removal from bodily existence, little was known of what was possible from that place, especially after many long ages of unsuperintended imprisonment.

Dorluc had at first placement in 'The Land', as he referred to it, almost gone mad from his apparent inability to have any intercourse in the tangible Worlds. It was only after long empty ages of pure consciousness that he had begun to see that there were other potentialities here in his new home. He discovered an oversight on the part of his mentors—the Magic of the Balance could be accessed even from The Land! At first there was only a small amount of power that was available. He found that he could view the temporal Worlds through a device (the view screen) The Old Ones had given him—and more! He did this by a great effort of his mental strength.

Before he had been exiled, he had been studying the use of telepathy and telekinesis through the magic of the first rudimentary parts of the *Passwords of Promise* that his level within the tiers of the Old Ones permitted him to have access to. In his rage at discommendation and disembodiment, he had failed in the early stages of formless life to explore his non physical opportunities. But eventually, instead of lamenting his physical limitation, he grew to accept it and enjoy a different, powerful effectiveness. The power of the Magic would allow him, with proper study and practice, at the very least, communication. At the most, influence and great manipulative abilities. It was an indirect language of conscious manipulation. It eventually proved very satisfactory to his otherwise total ostracism that had so far trammeled and frustrated him in this place.

After many ages he had honed his skills till they were as instinctual as breathing. His spirit life was elated. He tried to recall the physical form he once had, but could only intellectually remember as a word the concept and not the essential mechanisms of his corporeal life. He felt an emptiness in this area of corporeal knowledge. It angered him to lose what he thought were probably wonderful pleasures. His only joy now was to live more vicariously through the others he could watch from his view screen.

He found it odd how he could no longer 'feel' the meanings of all of his words. He was like one who had never seen color. It could be explained or defined only as far as the intellectual terms of language provided, but not in any way that demanded a physical experiential component. Once Dorluc had lost his flesh, he also lost the realm of the unique anthropomorphic component of cognition. It gradually left him. The ghosts of his corporeal understanding faded. He felt the agony, the loss and then nothing but rage. During this last stage he discovered his abilities to use the Magic of the Balance. It was like rebirth. He could replace his emptiness with its power. Steadily he grew in knowledge and the mysteries of the Magic, but it was not enough. The more he acquired, the more it reminded him of his unfair loss of temporal existence. He sought for a way to use the Magic to break free of this place. It should be possible he concluded. All he needed was greater knowledge of the use of this force.

The Magic was a pure energy maintained in a Balance. Once tapped, it linked every being past, present, or future to a shared consciousness. It was not of this world, but rather the fiber of the Worlds. It was spatial. Through this linking, Dorluc or any other, could sense those actively connected to it. At the beginning of his exile he was alone. Though his followers had also been exiled to The Land, Dorluc was not aware of where or if they could communicate. Eventually Dorluc discovered them through the Magic, and gathered them to him. They were shown the basics of what Dorluc had learnt and were soon able to be companions to him. Gradually they had built a little 'mental' community, where they existed linked together.

This additional mental strength helped. It enabled Dorluc to add greatly to the scope of the view screen. Not only could he watch the other worlds and search for any being, tapping into the Magic, it was soon powerful enough to allow him to influence or communicate with any of those beings that he could view. He became both encouraged that he might acquire his physical form again and more enraged that he no longer had it.

All of Dorluc's activity and constant linking to the Magic also caused a drain. A draining that soon drew the attention of another — Wakan. Wakan was also of the Old Ones. He had been the secret accomplice of Dorluc. Dorluc had never given him away, even after his punishment for attempting to misuse the *Passwords of Promise*. After the Old Ones had gone on, Wakan set up a mechanism whereby he remained strongly linked to the Magic and could communicate with those of the World's powerful and knowledgeable enough to connect to the Magic. He had tried to contact Dorluc once he was placed in the Land of No Form, but Dorluc was not knowledgeable enough, or able enough, to understand or realize this potentiality. Wakan had given up trying, just as Dorluc was starting to learn of his own connection and use of the Magic, as there were always tiny rifts, drains and changes within the Magic of the Balance. It was not until the level and constancy of the drain had been maintained for a substantial period that any notice was paid by Wakan toward Dorluc.

The Balance of the Worlds was boring to him and the secrecy of his role needed to be maintained. It was forbidden to attempt what he had done by creating a portal between the Worlds and the next zone. If it was discovered by his overuse, then he would find himself dealt with and punished as Dorluc had been. He hastily gave up on any notion of finding any, of the old Worlds, to help him to find the Key and *Passwords*. In order to find these items, it required that the searcher be one of physical form and a constituent of the Worlds. This was a protection beyond the hiding of the items, and the moles within the Chosen Ones that lay stealthily dormant and always ready to awaken and act. There was little fear on Wakan's part of any other competitor, except for Dorluc, who wanted the treasures. By the time the inhabitants of the temporal Worlds were advanced enough to discover the knowledge and reason for their existence, they would understand and respect the power they represented. They would leave the Key, the *Passwords*, and the Worlds behind, as was meant to be, then continue on, as the Old Ones in their turn had, to the next zone. It was the way. Dorluc was the only other source of threat and help for Wakan; the only other outcast who understood the power of the Key and *Passwords*. The only other corrupted by their Magic to the *Evil* element of the Balance. The other who wished and lusted after the secrets of invincibility.

Originally, Wakan had turned to Dorluc as his only hope, but that had proven ineffectual. After the discovery of the plot to secure the secrets and use them for their own gain, Dorluc and his followers had been punished. They had failed the test of the temptation of possessing the secrets. It was then that the leaders of Old Ones, the Ydnew, for the first time in the history of the Worlds realized that these secrets must be hidden away and protected from discovery or use by any. The secrets were never to be used. In fact, that was part of the greatest knowledge that one could possess. It was a difficult concept to comprehend. The secret's greatest power was Balance: being able to discover their existence and possess their knowledge, and though tempted, never use their Magic to interfere with the natural sequence of the Balance. It was through adherence to this principle that progression was accomplished beyond this temporal world to the next zone. It was a final test of deservedness. One which, if failed, would set back all advances made by all beings of the Worlds, and place them all into a chaotic reversal to darker ages.

There was a Balance to be maintained. It was a forgiving Balance, but it would not withstand tampering at the level that these secrets could provide. This was one reason why, upon this enlightenment, the Ydnew had put such limitations upon the distribution of the secrets of invincibility. It was too dangerous to risk the temptations that were revealed by their discovery.

Everyone within the Old One's society had accepted their wisdom without question, except Dorluc, his followers, and covertly Wakan. In time, myth developed amongst those of Dorluc's order. A myth of the greatness of the Magic as presented by the secrets, grew. These few believed that the secrets were being unfairly maintained and used by the Ydnew, the upper tier of their society. They tried continually to solicit more to their ranks. The Ydnew in the end reluctantly routed out those who continued these myths, thereby threatening the Balance. They attempted to reason and were forgiving, but they soon learned that even they, with their sophistication and sagacity, were not all immune to cancerous temptation of the *Evil* part of the Balance that the secrets would eventually in any hands, virulently lead.

After the Ydnew discovered what they felt were all the co-conspirators and completed their administration of their punishments, they decided to hide away this knowledge by an elaborate system of checks within checks that would not permit even them from knowing the whereabouts of 'their' hiding. The secrets had been divided into three elements and hidden, their concealment protected. All of the Old Ones now felt that all inhabitants of the Worlds would be secure and safe; that there were no longer any conspirators for power amongst them or the Worlds.

Peaceful life returned again until the rise of Ho and the Separation War. This was the first real testing of the protection system of the Old Ones. Ho had learnt of the Key through the writings, similar to Merm, except that he was not as well versed in the tongue of the ancient Gott as was Merm. Ho had misinterpreted and paid no heed to the warnings. He did not feel they had any significance. He was obsessed with the power that the Key would give to him. He did not have the intellect to avoid the pitfalls of the Magic. Nor was Dorluc able to strongly influence. This may have been a result of Dorluc's infancy in the use of his linking to the Magic. After all, this had been the first occasion to attempt to reestablish himself from The Land. He had not yet made stable his new found talents. He had not been working well with Wakan as a unified force. It had been more hit and miss. They both distrusted the other and the outcome of their misgivings was the consummate failure of Ho. Afterwards both of these *Evil* agents resolved not to allow their mutual uneasiness to prevent them from taking full advantage of the next opportunity, whenever it arrived! In the relatively short time between Ho and Merm, much refinement had been made in the partnership and the use of the Magic.

One large improvement was made to reduce the amount of drain to a minimal, when the Magic was in use by the *Evil*. This had been a real concern by Wakan. He did not want to alert or trip any alarms that would bring the Old Ones upon him. He knew that eventually they would be aroused, but by then he hoped the Key and *Passwords* would be in his control, and that the Old Ones then would be at a tremendous disadvantage. He would have more power and invincibility. Wakan through his knowledge of the upper tiers was able to explain more efficient ways to access the Magic. Dorluc found the improvements allowed him less effort and was able to longer apply his influence from his imprisonment to the Worlds. He was also shown a way to monitor the Magic for all drains including his own. At any moment that the drain became too strong he was alerted and could cease using the power until it was evened out. There was no longer the need to be concerned of discovery by others within the Balance.

Together, consciously united and combining their abilities, they could find the Key, and *Passwords*. Dorluc, even from banishment, could strongly and safely link with Wakan from inside the Magic. They then would use the secrets of invincibility to become indomitable and rule the Worlds in immortal corporeal form. No one, not even the Old Ones would be able to stop them after the Key and the *Passwords* were in 'his' control. Wakan and Dorluc each thought: 'his', since after the hidden item's uncovering and delivery, both planned to dispose of the other. Wakan had no desire to share anymore than he had to with Dorluc, nor Dorluc with Wakan.

They each did not want to risk keeping another of the Old Ones powers nearby; another that could be close enough and strong enough to make a true challenge.

Being alerted now by Merm's calling was not what Dorluc had expected. He realized that the Jardians were in the Caverns and that Merm had chased after them and entered the Zone. He did not expect there to be any other complications, and had been busy with future plans. He had not fully appreciated the assistance that these thieves were receiving from the depths of Magic. It was Wakan who had assisted Merm at the last moment in the Cavern of Three, not Dorluc.

Everything had happened so fast. Wakan had seen his opportunity to cut Dorluc out of their partnership. He believed that by intervening at this point on Merm's behalf in the Cavern of Three, he could acquire the Key and avoid its sharing with Dorluc. Though the *Passwords* had been placed into the Keeper's care, they were still retrievable with the Key.

In his greed Wakan had influenced Merm far too hard. Wakan had been too long not of corporeal form, and though it did not concern him personally anymore, he had neglected to be cautious for Merm's physical well being. He had seen the one thief with the Key go through the Tunnel of Light, and preparing to...he was not certain of what, just that here was a chance to get custody of the Key. He did not want to miss the moment. He had given Merm a tremendous push of influence. Under these circumstances with Merm's adrenaline already surging, the additional energy from Wakan clouded Merm's instincts of survival and prevented him from slowing in time to stop before going over the edge of the Tunnel opening. This was a surprise not only to Merm, but also the thief, who, being in the way was pushed over as well. Wakan's vehemence had caused exactly what he had not wanted: the losing of the Key to the river! The sobering of this actualization placed Wakan in a quandary. He would require Dorluc's power to combine with his own in order to save Merm and thereby get the Key.

When Dorluc became alerted, it was through the sensing of the fear from Merm's calling. Dorluc immediately beckoned his followers to come to the view screen room. Once there, they all saw Merm and the thief struggling through their abysmal fall, on the screen. They all without word, linked their magic by clasping hands, allowing Dorluc to focus his mind and channel their combined power on Merm. Before Dorluc could connect however, an opaque cloud appeared in the room and an image was becoming visible. This startled the others who had never before witnessed its appearance and were not aware of a partnership within their *Evil*. They were silent as they watched and listened. Dorluc was not pleased at this revealing. He scowled and before the image was fully formed, gathered his senses and angrily ordered everyone to leave. Just as the last one had left the room, the image became clear.

"Why are you here? This is not the time. There is trouble. How am I to account for your intrusion?" Dorluc did not wait for answers, but fired the words at Wakan.

"The Gott has followed after the thief. He has foolishly jumped into the abyss from the Cavern in Tika. I was watching, but was not able to prevent it. We must join together and save the Key. We need to combine our strength within the Magic."

Wakan was not about to reveal the truth. There would be no way for Dorluc to know otherwise, unless he had been viewing in the screen. Wakan thought that unlikely. Dorluc would have been loosely connected to Merm at the very least, and would reluctantly accept Wakan's 'watching excuse', since he himself was probably secretly connected to Merm without notifying Wakan. Dorluc would not like the idea, but would be forced to accede to the logic of Wakan's watching. In a way, Wakan had been correct to watch. Dorluc would not be able, without loosing face, to admit that he was secretly linked, but by all rights he should have been. From Dorluc's perspective, Wakan's action may have saved the situation!

"What!" Dorluc would not reveal that he was secretly linked. He instantly decided to avoid the situation. He knew that Wakan was not being truthful, and that he would know that his linking would have been done. To admit it now, this way, was playing into Wakan's hand. Dorluc would not give Wakan that satisfaction, of playing into his hand. The most important issue now, was to secure Merm from any danger that would stop them from getting the Key.

"Is that what this," he pointed a skeletal finger at the images on the view screen, "is?"

"Yes." Wakan understood.

"Then let us join together." Dorluc understood.

There was no more speech. Slowly Dorluc

walked toward and into the cloud, till he also was surrounded by its gaseousness. Gradually both images blended together. Then came the ancient tongue repeated over and over, growing louder and louder creating a spiral shape. The words, along with the images, began to blur:

"Wru ho lik hy fut! Wru ho lik hy fut! Wru ho lik hy fut! Wru ho lik hy fut! Wru ho lik hy fut! Wru ho lik hy fut! Wru ho lik hy fut! Wru ho lik hy fut! Wruho lik hy fut! Wru ho likhy fut! Wru holik hy fut! Wruho likhy fut! Wruholikhyfut"

At the exact moment when the words had blurred into sounding as one, there was a flash. Dorluc and Wakan were one. There was a moment of silence in the room. Then the cloud disappeared and there alone was standing Dorluc.

Or rather Dorluc with the energy of Wakan inside. It would have taken too much energy to maintain his visual presence here in the Worlds; an energy which would have become noticeable within the Magic during the amount of time that was needed to save the Key. This also would make it easier for Dorluc with his followers.

Dorluc opened his eyes. He felt stronger. He called out to his followers. There was a shuffling and then they were back and standing around the view screen. The two figures on the view screen were still falling.

"We will join together again," he did not feel the need to explain the cloud, and they would not question. "We will use our energy to protect the Gott from his fall. Quickly. Push your thoughts. Harder! We must have the Jardian as well."

With the joining, Dorluc and Wakan shared most of their thoughts, except for the ones that each shielded before the joining. Dorluc was instantly aware of the situation that Merm was now in, and also understood all that had occurred within the Cavern of Three. All except Wakan's intervening. He knew of the disposition of the *Passwords* and that the one Jardian was attempting to keep the Key from them. If he managed to enter the water below, Dorluc knew that the Key would be lost. The Jardian would be pulled into the depths of the river, and he with the Key taken with the current till they would be lost and thereby protected.

The river held many mysteries. Like the Moonfruit Pine of the lower forest, it had the Magic flowing within its great mass. Dorluc was aware in his joining with Wakan of this factor. But even Wakan was not privy to the scope or nature of its power. He was not completely knowledgeable of what the Magic was, just that within it there was a power of sensing. The river was powerful and originated deep within the mountains of Tika. It was the river of the Old Ones and fed the great Lake of Choices. It had been rumored by the outside Worlds that the Pass River contained demons; that these Demons protected an ancient treasure of the Old Ones. They did not know that this treasure was the Key and the *Passwords of Promise*.

The river had been given the power of sense. It was a limited power. The water would sense for the Key and those charged with its protection. This was all part of the system set by the Ydnew through their final understanding of the secrets of invincibility. By the time the Old Ones had reached their highest Tiers, and uncovered the secrets of invincibility, they learnt that part of this knowledge was that all the elements of the Worlds had within them a life source. Some were more advanced or sophisticated, but all had this Magic of the Balance within them.

These were the 'spirits' or 'demons' alluded to by the more primitive societies of the Worlds. Though they were 'primitive' because of their inability to 'understand' or explain the workings of their Worlds, they were in a way more 'knowledgeable' than the societies that felt they were better because they had begun to unfold or conquer the wisdom of their existence. The primitive societies in a way were more accurate in 'primitive' explanations, respect and superstitions. They at least appreciated, though misinterpreted, the more fundamental natural realities of the elements surrounding them. For the more 'wise' had foolishly lost or let go, in their arrogance and self aggrandizement, of the Balance that was necessary to their well being and continued growth in the Worlds. They tended to exploit the natural elements as unimportant and plentiful.

Everything in the Worlds was also connected and a part of the Magic of the Balance. Like the

Moonfruit, the river would help to protect and give safe passage to the Chosen Ones and the Key if detected within the zone of Tika. Once Julian entered the water here, he would be cushioned and the impact absorbed, enabling him to survive the fall. Outside of Tika, the river had less personality. It would be able to detect the Chosen and the Key, but only be able to offer a minimal resistance to any trying to harm them. The Magic of the Key, with its linking within the Balance, would provide, to its beholder, any other help needed to escape the *Evil*.

This would not be the case for Merm. When he hit the river it would be like hitting solid ground unless he was helped by someone or thing. The *Evil* would help. It would not let that happen. Dorluc and his followers were beginning the process to save Merm.

Just as Dorluc had pulled Julian under the surface of the river at the crossing, he could reverse his power to soften Merm's falling. Merm would survive the fall as long as the combined Magic of Dorluc and Wakan was strong enough. It was easier to pull under and add to already existing motions, but resisting and changing the velocity of an established momentum, was much less predictable. Dorluc hoped there was enough magic between them to prevent this disaster.

The thought of the Key lost, after being so close, was galling. The amount of drain in the Magic, awakening of the moles, and ignition of other tools of protection, of which he was not aware, was dangerous.

The moles were a series of dormant beings scattered within their hosts throughout the Worlds. Through the Magic of the Balance some of their fundamental elements had been altered to speed up their growth in the knowledge of the Balance. There was a spark placed deep within each of them, that under the correct circumstances would ignite them to protect the Worlds. After the threat was gone, the host of the mole would lose almost all memory of the awakening. A very small residual of knowledge would remain, but it was not enough on a single awakening to be of concern. The hosts would remain ignorant of the knowledge. They would feel that something had changed. They would have begun the journey towards the knowledge and invincibility, but it would be at the most rudimentary level. The more times there were of awakening, the greater the residual memory of awareness became. Eventually when the threat or threats reached more extended periods of duration, the hosts would begin to accumulate the knowledge and remember the occurrences of the awakening within them. Eventually they would become conscious of the Magic. From that point on, they would be initiated and securely on the early path of Magic, like the Old Ones had once been. The circle of growth would continue, and the new Chosen would become the Old Ones in their time. Once they had passed the test of deservedness and became Chosen, there would be no returning back to unawareness of awakening. It was a long process, with many ups and downs and varying duration's of recall and loss of access to the Magic. These individuals were on the initial path toward invincibility.

After the recent skirmish between the Gotts and the Worlds, the Old Ones might already be preparing to intervene more substantially. Dorluc was not sure if this was a possibility, but assumed, with what he now knew from Wakan's sharing, that there were many powers and moles of whom he and Wakan were ignorant.

"How far had the awakenings progressed? Had it stirred the Old Ones or just used the existing Magic of the various aspects of the system of protection?"

Dorluc hoped that it had not gone farther.

Though he was not informed as to this system, his sharing with Wakan provided glimpses of such things. If this attempt failed, he did not want to jeopardize his prospects of trying again at a later time, with another agent.

Within the Key's Magic was the illusionary magic. The same as Dorluc had given to Merm to use. When called upon it could project both the imagery and sounds of whatever level of magic that was required. Unknown to Dorluc, this was what had occurred during the end of the Gott invasion of the North when Julian had uttered the words and called upon this power. The Old Ones had not really responded. They were not at that time aware of the dangers. It was the Magic of the system of protection that was being used. There should be no need for them to be distracted. There should be enough deterrents and magic within the system. It would take greater dangers and action to signal them. Ones that, till Julian's leap into the abyss, had not yet transpired.

Dorluc stopped his wandering thoughts and concentrated upon the falling Merm. He felt the powerful linked magic flowing through him from Wakan.

Merm was still trying to catch the thief. They

had both fallen at least a third of the distance into the canyon abyss. He was getting used to the fall. He was so close to the Southlander that he could, even through the force of the passing air, smell the fear from him. He pulled harder again through the nothingness. Just as he was about to grab hold of the thief, a series of events happened so quickly that it was hard for Merm to understand. There came the voice of his dreams, Dorluc, followed by an image that was falling with him about a length away and between him and the thief.

"I will help you. Get the Key!" Dorluc projected his image and thoughts to Merm. The rest of his energy was being applied to the softening of Merm's fall.

Merm was stunned. Before he could respond, he noticed that the thief was falling faster than he. Somehow Merm was slowing in his descent! He wanted to call out for whatever was slowing him to stop.

"NO!" ran throughout Merm's being.

Dorluc heard the words, and wondered why the doomed Gott would resist help. He looked to the Jardian and then realized that he had no control over the fall of the thief, even though he had extended the combined power over both of the falling figures. He clasped harder onto the ones next to him in the room.

"Harder!" he called out.

Everyone in the room strained to extend the energy of their magic to include the thief. Still nothing was forthcoming. They could see the rapidly separating figures in the view screen.

"What is wrong? Which of you is not helping?" Dorluc lashed out at his followers in the room who were all linked and obviously intimidated. There were a few moments of puzzlement. "Again! Let us all work!"

Again they all channeled their power and tried to spread their influence over the thief. Nothing. The distance between Merm and the Jardian was now three lengths. Merm was agonizing over the gradual distancing. He struggled more and more to stop the gap widening. He could not reach the Key.

Dorluc strained. Still the gap widened. He could not exert the influence over the Jardian.

"It must be the Key. The Key was protecting the Jardian. The power of the Magic is strong amongst him."

Dorluc began to consider his next steps over the remaining moments before the river was reached. The thief would hit first. Then the Key would be lost! Merm would be safe, but the opportunity lost.

'They' were all stunned. Dorluc decided in his panic to give one final surge within the Magic and push toward the thief. He closed his eyes and with his followers concentrated upon the thief.

Merm began to cry out in his frustration. "Noooooooooooooo!" echoed within the canyon abyss. He knew now that he would not be able to reach the Southlander before he entered the river. His body twisted as he struggled to keep a constant watch on the Southlander. He would follow after him once in the water and try to catch up with this robber of the Key.

As he went through all these rapid events, Merm was filled with mixed emotions. Doubt began to swell within him. There were so many influences happening within the smallest instants. As he slowed and twisted, Merm lost his view of the Southlander for a blink of a moment and as instantly, the Southlander vanished with a sudden burst of white light into what appeared to be an opening and closing, a ripping in the sky, as if it were just a piece of fabric. It opened, sucked in the Southlander, then closed. There was no trace of the Southlander or any proof that anything had just happened or that he had ever been there. It was over before they could react. He was gone.

Dorluc had witnessed this event. The Jardian was gone. "But where? What had happened?"

The only figure left on the screen was the Gott. Dorluc averted some of his concentration to direct the view screen to scan for the other. There was no result. There was no trace. Merm was the only figure the screen showed along with the sound of the river growing in volume. Two thirds of the distance to it was now traveled. In a few more moments, Merm would be submerged within its choppy rage. There was no time to consider the Jardian. There was no other option. He must act to save Merm.

"What a fool to jump!" Dorluc muttered reproachingly.

♀ ♪ ♪ ♪ ♪ ♩ ☥ ☰ 〰♪ 👁 👁 👁 ♈

"No! Don't go! Not again! Please!" Lenore's heart ached again as she pleaded, but another pulse of a beam from the *Evil* brought her quickly back to the reality of her nightmare. She had to act immediately. There was no other way. She would do as she had been told.

With her arms shielding her, she struggled to her knees under the force of the *Evil's* beam. It was a strain. She was drawing upon the deepest resources within her; the deepest parts, where those within her lay dormant. Lenore was not sure what to make of this. She felt a surge of strength from those depths, she was in disbelief—"Surely this was just a bizarre ingredient of this dream? This was not *really* a part of her!"

There was no time to ponder. There was only incredulous acceptance, "When I awake from this nightmare," she mused, "everything will be as it always has been."

As this new strength grew within Lenore, the exchange between her and the image in the cloud was heightened. Slowly Lenore had managed to stand and was countering the *Evil's* power. With this initial success, she became even more determined to prevail, though she knew the struggle was far from won. One wrong placement of her feet and she would still be over the edge and defeated.

"Shruu jik doi!" came the ancient tongue, followed by a stronger beam of repelling magic from Lenore's outstretched fingertips. The *Evil* faltered, being caught off guard by Lenore's sudden recovery. Lenore attempted to step forward away from the edge. She was stopped. Three sudden bursts from within the cloud beat upon her.

"Your mediocre tricks will not work here. You are still no match. Over! Over into the nothingness!" a raspy voice came from the cloud.

A bead of perspiration rolled from Lenore's

right temple and on down her soft facial skin as she felt herself teeter backwards. She strained and called out in her mind for help. Though no words were spoken, the *Evil* had heard:

"There is no one to help you now. Give in to me." There was a change of tone to the *Evil's* voice, "Give in to me now and I will save you."

If he could win this female over, he would be able to acquire another to strengthen his side. He would then absorb her magic and discard her. "Do not resist any longer. I do not wish you harm. Together we can..."

"NooooOOOOOO!"

It was a wild vociferation coming from deep within her. It was gut wrenching.

"No o o O O O O O O! No o o O O O O O!"

With each outcry came a series of powerful blasts. Three times she cried out. On the third, she took one strong sturdy step forward:

"You will not have them!"

As she pushed against the *Evil*, a section of her subconscious thoughts suddenly went to her brother. Where was he? Was he alive? She called to him.

66 *J* ulian." came the voice. It was being whispered, as if someone was leaning very close and speaking so that only he would hear the secret.

"*Julian*, you know the way. It is inside."

Till now, there had been such complete silence in the zone of the shaft, that Julian was a little bewildered. He wondered if this was just another memory or dream about to start its replay. There was no way of knowing. This time however, instead of tensing up and being pulled along by the memory jump, Julian became more assertive. He welcomed its speedy commencement. He had nothing to gain anymore by being apprehensive. He wanted answers,

"Who...where are you? Is there someone there, or am I dreaming?"

Julian was fatigued and frustrated. He was nearing his limits to withstand the bizarre manipulating magic of the Labyrinths. He wanted to believe that he had really heard the voice. A voice in a place of no perceptible noises. But the sound was not coming from outside, rather within him. The voice was strange and old. It echoed. Not the echo of one voice as it reverberated, but the sound of three separate voices all intertwined and overlapping. Each voice was saying the same words but in a different texture and at slightly offset times which gave a false sense of an echo:

"Julian, the way is clear. Follow what you know. It is before you. Choose."

This was definitely not a memory being replayed. It was a familiar voice, but one that Julian had never heard in this place. His spirits raised. Perhaps there was help available to him here? He was not alone.

"Choose what?!" Julian bellowed out, though there was no sound. "I don't understand. What way? What do I know? Is this real or am I just imagining it all?"

"You have access to a powerful magic. Do not fight what you know to be true. You have used it before." the voice was confident.

"When?" as Julian replied he considered. During his escape through the Burning Forest, and his meeting of Quei and Thodox, he realized he had used the magic to create his disappearing enroute to the Dwellers' home. He had thought at the time that it was merely a trick. He never made more of it. He now wondered why he had never bothered to question more of this before.

"Why?" he heard himself thinking out loud.

"Yes...you do remember." It was as if the voice had heard the memory of Julian's thoughts.

"The river crossing. The disappearing in the forest. It is from the same source. Use that same magic now." as the voice conversed it was becoming more singular in its nature. Its reverberating diminishing. It was becoming more narrowed in tone and texture; a texture that had a definite *maleness* to it.

"But I don't want to vanish now. I need to save myself from that Gott and the abyss. I have the Key." Julian raised his hand to indicate his possession of the item, as if someone were present with him and watching.

"It is the same. You should not yet be here. You need to be in the other place. You have arrived here unknowingly and must return to finish what *we* are promised to do. You know of what I speak." the other 'echoes' were clearly gone. The voice was now wholly male and as he listened, Julian noted an intimacy to its sound. He felt this intimacy as he continued to communicate.

"What do you mean?" Julian spoke. For the moment he had managed to overlook the torment of his passage in the endless shaft, by trying to identify the voice.

"You do not have long here. You must hurry. Look within. Close out the confusion. Think, as you have before, of where you *will* be. Transfer your thought. Allow the power within to direct your path. It will feel right. You will know. Choose it. Commit to it. Remove the fear." the voice was instructing and starting to fade. It had delivered the message.

"Where are we? How?" Julian felt as though

he were a young Jardian again. The voice had a
soothing nostalgic quality. It made him feel as if
he were safe and in his home in Jard. The same
way his... "Father?" he blurted out, "Is it you?
Please don't go."

The voice strengthened, "Julian, there is no
more time. You must act quickly. Soon you will
understand all that there is to know. Do not
question further. I am your father and I am not.
I am much more than you can know. It is too
early for your awakening to these things. There
is much that you need to learn, but now you
must fulfill your destiny. *We* must not spend
these remaining precious few moments on other
matters. There will be another occasion to
meet."

"But I want to know more. What am I to do?
How? What is this place? Am I dead?" Julian
began to babble. He was frightened of being left
alone in this place. He was so full of indecisive-
ness.

The voice recognized this and comforted:

"All that you need to know is inside. Search
your deepest parts. You are not yet dead and
will, in a way beyond your imaginings, never die.
'We' are always here. Remember all the tales
and songs you were enthralled with as a young

Jardian. Not the words but the imagery and the music. This is the way of the Chosen. There is great Magic in those things. They will unlock the power you have been given to accomplish *our* duty."

"Our duty? Who is..." Julian was cut short. It was posturing, for he knew as he uttered these few words that there *was* a duty. He had begun to understand this since the tea and re acquaintance with Darla in Jard. His mind lapsed and a brief replay of the memory overtook him:

He was in his garden with Eruinn, Thiunn and Darla.

"What's happening?" called out one of the youngsters.

"DO NOT BE CONCERNED CHOSEN ONE!" It was an ancient voice, and all four had privately heard it.

Julian began to notice that the jewels in the Darla's sword were glowing brighter and brighter, and that Darla herself was being enveloped by a whitish egg shaped glow, like an aura. It kept growing till finally the sword stopped glowing and merely hummed.

"Do not be concerned Chosen Ones!" Now the voice emanated from Darla herself. It was her own voice but stronger in tone and

impact, similar to the echoed voice being presented to him here in the shaft:

> *"The door is past, the Evil begins.*
> *Awaken! Begin! Four shall defend.*
> *All was forgotten, now comes true.*
> *The Key and Passwords remain to be freed.*
> *Return with your birthright the Balance they need."*

Six notes pierced through them and then there was sudden blackness! It was night, and he was in the garden in Jard.

Julian in the memory, was thinking of his father and the long talks and stories he used to laboriously tell, always asking his son if he would swear to do his part when the time came. Julian thought his father meant family responsibilities and the passing on of the craft. But now he reasoned that the Key was also a part of the responsibility. He had heard stories of ancient magic and the important mission to protect the Balance. He now realized that they were not just stories.

"There is no time to waste. Do not distract yourself from your purpose." the voice interjected, thereby causing the memory to end its replay.

Julian was conscious again of being in the shaft

and his present predicament. He felt that this memory had somehow been altered, changed in some way to help him understand better and act more quickly. He noticed an impatience in the voice:

"These things are within you. You know more than you wish to accept. Trust in yourself. Do not ask the questions. Rely on the feelings inside. You are in a place of temporary safety, but you do not yet belong here in this zone. You must leave. Your thoughts are not yet strong enough for this place. Return to your home. Understand the meaning of the memories. Just as before in the river, we will help you."

Without warning, a blinding flash lit up a forward area of the void, as another shaft entered the darkness of the Labyrinths, close to Julian's own shaft's track. Resultantly, Julian was distracted and did not notice the leaving of the voice that he believed was his father. After the startlement of the other shaft's passing, Julian returned his attention to his conversation with the voice. He responded:

"I remember many times when you sang the old tunes to me. But I do not remember the details. They were just tales." Julian waited for a response but felt only a silence within his mind.

He was alone again. It was as if he had been disconnected from an ancient shared consciousness; a consciousness of many generations. He had not had any notion of this at the time of conversing, but now he believed that there had been an accessing to a vast powerful collective of ancestral knowledge. It had come in a glimpse, but now it was gone. He panicked, "Father? Father!" No one answered.

He lay stunned in the shaft, running over the jilted conversation. He was confused and not certain anymore as to the identity of the voice. He still wanted to believe it was his father's voice that had spoken with him, but could not explain the other echoes that had been present with it. There was no explication he could offer. Nor was he in any type of tangible frame of mind, in this place, that could help him work it out. It was pointless trying to pursue this line of thinking. He tried to distract himself from it by recalling the words of his father's intercourse, focusing on particular phrases.

"You do not have long here. You must hurry. Look within. Close out the confusion. Think **as you have before** of where you will be. Transfer your thought. **Allow the power within to direct** your path. It will **feel right**. Choose it. Commit to it. **Remove the fear**. There is no time. These things are **within you**. You know more than you wish to accept. **Trust in yourself**. Do not ask the questions. Rely on the feelings inside. Do not distract yourself from OUR purpose. You are in a place of temporary safety, but you do not yet belong here. You must leave. Your thoughts are not yet strong enough for this place. **Return to your home. Just as before in the river, we will help** you." These words of his father replayed instantly. They flashed before him. He whispered the stressed phrases:

"...*as you have before...Allow the power within to direct...feel right...Remove the fear...within you...Trust in yourself...Return to your home. Just as before in the river, we will help.*"

Julian became absorbed by the imagery that these words conjured. He fell into the memories they held, and waited for the replay of their recall. This time there was no fear of the jumping into the memories, instead, an eagerness was swelling.

His mind turned to the memory of the river crossing. He recalled again the strength of its current, his powerlessness amidst its pull. Yet he had overcome these things! What had he done at that event to escape the pull of the water? He re-lived the submersion and the strange sensation of a life within the wetness. The memory was re-playing. This time, Julian would learn from it and not let the fear of reliving the sequences distract him. The words he had spoken upon its first replaying in these Labyrinths of Light sur-faced: "There is something more to this water unlike the water in Jard. This water has a pres-ence. There is a silent entity within it."

He was bobbing again in the rough water of the river and gasping for air! Thodox and Quei were still running along the bank trying to keep pace with him. He would not last if he couldn't get to a bank soon. Every time his head went below the surface, it was longer till he popped back up. He **would not** *die! Julian was being swept far away! Under he went again, and again and again…this last time he failed to surface. Julian was go-ing down deeper. It was not right! The change in the river had been too sudden and Julian's efforts should have been bringing at least some tiny result! A tremendous panic was taking hold.* **This shouldn't be happen-ing!**

When he had gone under and was held in

place, preventing him from rising to the surface, a voice spoke clearly to him,

*"**Do not be afraid**. It is the Evil that holds you. Take hold of the Key."*

*Julian fumbled to find the Key that he had tied into his pocket. Taking hold of it meant giving up one hand that might pull him to the surface. **He trusted the voice** and did what it had directed.*

Julian found the Key which was still where he had hidden it in his pocket. In using his arms to search, the force under the river completely overtook his body. He was being sucked deeper into its depths! He had taken hold of the Key in hope of some Magical rescue. None ensued. His breath was lean, and his mind was screaming out for fresh oxygen. Just when he thought he would explode, a voice was again present,

"Do not be afraid. Allow the moment to pass. You will not perish."

*Julian had no other option but do as the voice beckoned. **He relaxed** and allowed his being to go limp.*

*"**Think of the surface. Think of the bank.**"*

*He complied with the voice. **He imagined that he was sitting on the bank on the other*** *side of the narrows where the boulders were to allow the crossing. **More and more he saw himself there.** It was strange. **The more he visualized himself actually there, the more comfortable he was in the water.** His concern for fresh air was diminishing. This encouraged him to concentrate more till the only reality in his mind was of him on the other side of the river sitting on shore. It became more and more real. He closed his eyes. **More and more he imagined the scene.** Soon he did not even hear the muffled sound of the water all around him, or even its feel. He concentrated further. **He actually began to hear the cool night breeze and feel the air blowing against his wet body.** He thought to open his eyes, but was afraid to break the vision, his only hope of relief!*

*He kept this up for what seemed a long time. Finally, he could not withstand the temptation to see where he had been pulled by the river. He opened his eyes—**he was sitting on the bank on the other side of the river!***

As this memory played through, a revelation struck Julian. It was so simple. It had been too uncomplicated to be taken seriously before now.

It had been so obvious, yet he had never before considered how he had managed his escape from the river crossing. He only briefly thought on it, having been too distracted by all the other following events. That was one rationalization. Or perhaps he was afraid and really didn't want to understand what had happened. His father was right. Now that there was a need he had begun to appreciate at a very rudimentary level, that there was much more to that episode than luck. Julian had called upon the Magic, though he didn't yet completely comprehend the process, the spark, that had illuminated his consciousness. It was no longer an instinctual occurrence, instead, there was a grasping of his inner ability to control or make outcomes happen. He had the insight:

The Labyrinths of Light were the Magic in its purest form. The Magic was like a brain in a delicate electro synaptic balance. Upset this delicate set of variables by affecting the Magic within its myriad of synaptic Labyrinths, such as the *Evil* would do with the Key and *Passwords*, and watch how unpredictable and precarious the result would be. The Magic, akin to a brain, was both: a most powerful tool and potentially a most destructive one, depending on the tampering within this delicate Balance.

"It was not luck!"

As the light within him sparked, the replaying of the memory ended. He was returned back into the awareness of the shaft and was for the first time, grinning. Though not fully cognizant of the where or what of this place, he now understood that it was not a place of the *Evil*. Somehow in the desperation of his falling into the abyss, Julian had tapped an inner magic, just like at the river. The tapping had been initialized by the process of calming and listening to a voice. He appreciated its roots:

"Do not be afraid... trust the voice... relax... Think of the..."

The solution was simple. Through accepting his fate, he could manage to maneuver a way around the expected outcome. He was more capable of using this influence, but was still uncomfortable about it. Though he was still confused about this zone, for the first time Julian felt as if he could 'maneuver' himself to safety.

"If only I could have more time with father. Just one more moment. There is much that I want to know."

Julian was still not quite ready to use his inner being to aid in his conscious tapping into the Magic to leave these Labyrinths.—LEAVE THIS

PLACE! The sudden impact of the abyss and treacherous river awaiting him in his own rightful other reality, sent a sobering chill down his spine of his pending mortality. He was still not confident of survival after leaving this nesting place. He began to slip back into a panic.

"No. I can't." he fearfully muttered. "I will not survive." he was speaking, he thought to himself.

There was a pause. The glow within his shaft brightened. There were not many more moments until the end. If no action was taken by Julian from this place, in the few moments before he would hit the bottom of the abyss in the canyon of the real other world, wherever that reality was now in relation to this zone, then he would remain in the shaft. But he would not last long there either. He was not yet ready to remain here. He did not have the ability to direct the course of the shaft to another 'real' world where he could play out his physical existence. He was not yet ready.

The shaft was a transitory place, not meant for prolonged interlopers. Eventually the jumping of memories would escalate, till finally it would drive him mad. He would perish. There would be no help for him here. It was a zone of passage into which no outside influence was permitted or possible. The Old Ones would never know. Only those of his ancestors within the Magic would know, for he would join them, and stand ready to help the next Stoneman.—But he was the only one! He had no offspring. Julian became distraught. He could not allow this end. He must fulfill his duty in *all* ways! He must do it on his own. There would be no supernatural intervention of the Old Ones, not at this level of threat to the Balance.

The Old Ones did not keep watch. They did not look constantly on as deities might to the Worlds. Instead, the system of protection that had been developed by them would steadily magnify to counter any threats to the Balance. The contingency of returning to the physical universe of the Worlds was kept only as a final, last resort option. If all other methods failed, then the Old Ones could personally and physically intervene. It was not however, their wish to do so, or so the legend went. They were not willing to prematurely return to the type of primitive conceptualization of these Worlds, especially as there was a system in place that could more than adequately provide protection. Also, the process of the threat and awakenings of not only the Chosen, but others, was a necessary part of learning. It would lead all the inhabitants of the Worlds to higher levels of peace, understanding, and of the values that would maintain a harmony or Balance.

The Balance, in order to remain, had to be maintained by the general informed and enlightened will of all inhabitants of the Worlds. It could not be arbitrarily forced into equilibrium by outsiders, or non residents. It fed off the energy of the shared desire of *all* those of the Worlds implicitly involved. It drew the Magic from every living aspect of those Worlds. Everyone shared, maintained, and was a part of its Balance. No external power could long manipulate that Balance. It was far too consuming. All energies must come from within its scope. To allow any outsider influence, would lead to the unwinding of the fabric of eternity. For energy taken from another part would create a weakening in that part, and an over strengthening in the other one to which it was applied. Neither part would be able to compensate for the imbalance 'that' intrusion and weakening thus created.

It was very intricate, and delicate. This was in part the secret of the Key and *Passwords*. By using them and causing imbalance it would cause even greater, more profound, damage. It would eventually undermine and annihilate every place, time, and being. There would be no stopping the unraveling. The Balance must, as a result, be maintained by those within each sphere of its particular influence, and tier. Everywhere it was maintained within that context; everywhere there then resulted: the Balance. Julian must complete his duty and prevent any further complications within this domain that would cause setbacks to all the corners of the Balance. The Old Ones knew all these things. It was up to those of the threatened Worlds, unless the complications proved insurmountable, to resolve these dangers.

Julian should access the Magic, draw from it, and through its power be guided by the others before. But he first had to use the power placed within him to initiate that process of awakening. He was preventing himself from taking this first conscious step. All had happened so quickly since his tea in Jard. He had not had time to internalize what was now being demanded. He was still in many ways a child. This next step presented unknown territory to him. He was reluctant to open any other new doors that he may not need to open and then the dilemma of dealing with their consequences. Julian had never liked the uncertainties associated with change. Given the chance, he would have followed his normal regular predictable existence, and never embarked upon this adventure. How he begrudged being involved in all of this!

"Please help me." he begged, still not willing to assume control over outcomes.

"JULIAN. JULIAN. THERE IS NOT MUCH TIME. YOU MUST ACT." the echoed voice returned. This time the maleness was less dominant. There was a more female quality to it.

"Father?"

"No Julian. You must do what you know. It has been long since we spoke. You were but new." the voice exuded empathy.

"I don't understand."

"Stop. Do not continue this way. You have the ability. Trust in your Magic. Relax. Think on the task. There is not much time. Act."

"But what if I can't. If I fail?"

"You will not. There is greater Magic than you can imagine within. Your duty is partially complete. Act. Complete that which is promised."

"But I never made the promise."

"You are bound by our oath. There is no longer a choice. You must act. Trust in your power. We will be with you, always."

"I am so confused"

"Julian, I am the one that gave life to the continuing of our promise. Julian, you will act now."

"Who are you?"

"Search your feelings of long ago. Feel the power of the glow."

"Mother?"

"I am here. Now you must act. Julian, the time is almost gone. Aaacct!" the voice faded away on the last word.

"No! Please stay." Julian was emotionally worn. "What is going on here?" he questioned this last voice, "Why must I go?"

He lay vacant with his eyes open, within his shaft. His heart was heavy and a lump grew in his throat. The effects of the shaft were increasing in intensity. He knew that he could not withstand for long these disorientating mental and emotional barrages. Whether the conversations were imagined or not, he could no longer reliably judge. It was far too implausible for his Jardian essence to understand. He could not count on what he thought or saw. He considered his situation. He was on the verge of a decision. He knew that he must take some action. It was time to complete his journey, while he was still capable of making this choice. He did not want to stay here anymore. Facing the abyss would be better than the incessant incoherency of these Labyrinths of Light. The voices, if they had been real, were correct. It was the required way to continue. He searched his being. He somehow sensed that he could trust these insights—now was the time to act. He must hurry!

- -

"Do not break the union. We will envelope him with our magic." Dorluc was concerned that he and his followers would not be able to protect Merm from this falling death. All in the room watched through the screen and channeled their power through Dorluc and around Merm.

"Why does he resist us?" just as Dorluc was questioning why Merm was struggling against their protective force, he saw that the Jardian was not within their grip. That was the reason for Merm's protest. But it was too late. Dorluc had no other course to follow. He had to maintain the protective envelope which had somehow not held onto the Jardian and allowed them to become more separated. There were only a few moments left. It would not be possible to break the protection on Merm and reach for the other. They would never be able to re-establish Merm's envelopment!

"Do not break the linking." repeated Dorluc as he watched the scene.

Shared within Dorluc, Wakan had also viewed this calamity. The answer to the quandary presented by the thief's escaping the hold, would be left until after the Gott was safe. This thief was obviously of great Magic. Just as abruptly as the thief had disappeared from Dorluc's view screen, he popped back into it. He had only been gone from view a few instants. Nothing could be done but watch. Dorluc was committed to his actions. The water of the river was now only a few lengths away. As soon as Merm was safely slowed so that the impact in the river would not harm him, Dorluc would then turn his wrath to the thief of the Key. He called out to his shared being, Wakan, to prepare for the capture of the thief when he fell into the river. There was no answer.

As Merm was finally enclosed within the power of the *Evil*, Wakan allowed a section of his being to wander within the Balance. He would investigate any unusual drains that might account for the abrupt escaping of the thief. At first there was nothing of note, then suddenly there it was, a surge. There was a new drain. Wakan pursued its source. It was coming from…a dreaming female. He decided to enter her dream and put an end to whatever part she had played in aiding the thief. Wakan did not realize that it was Lenore, the sibling of the thief!

Julian calmed himself from as much of the distraction as possible. He emptied his mind of the present fears that he held, concentrating on a feeling of well being and security. He tried to recapture the same state of mind that he had held while being pulled under the river at the crossing with Quei and Thodox. He concentrated. More and more he thought of being back in his own world. He visualized the canyons from whence he had just come. He imagined the cool damp air as it had rushed and rippled about him. He searched for an inner glow of contentment. More and more he centered his awareness.

Just as in the river at the crossing, he began to lose any awareness of the zone of the shaft. There were no more flashes of light or jumpings into memory. The confusion and abstraction of the Labyrinths within his thought was going. Slowly it diminished, then it was gone! He suddenly actually *felt* the wind and heard its deafening thunder as before he had entered the Labyrinths. His eyes were still closed. He did not want to disturb the process of his return, if it was indeed working. He concentrated.

- -

"You will not have them!" Lenore was steadily moving toward the cloud. She felt an urgency to find her brother. To help him. To lend him her strength. She did not understand, but was compelled forward to the completion of this goal.

Wakan had been enjoying their struggle. This female was strong in the Magic, but not as strong as he. She had only succeeded thus far, because of Wakan's current sharing of Magic with Dorluc to save Merm. As soon as that was accomplished, he could apply his full Magic against this female.

It was as the female approached and pressured, that the call from Dorluc arrived. "The thief is back. Quickly, now is our chance!"

Wakan instantly let go his combat with Lenore

and dissolved back into the Magic to return to Dorluc.

The fight terminated as unpredictably as it had commenced. Lenore watched from her sleep baffled as the cloud dissipated and the force within it went. She was relieved, but also at a loss. She realized that this was not a good omen. Her mind returned to her young ones and her brother. She screamed out his name: "**JULIAN!**" Everything went blank.

- - - - - - - - - - - - - - - - - - - -

Julian's efforts were proceeding as before at the river crossing en route to Tika. He was beginning to transfer back to his own world from the Labyrinths, though he was not exactly aware that this was occurring. He continued to concentrate; to relax the way he felt he had done during the previous occasions of his transference from danger. More and more he relaxed and let go, till finally he willingly let go his control of his being, giving over to an unknown powerful Magic. It soothed. Gradually his mind was tapping into the correct variables that would transport him away from the Labyrinths. He felt at peace, except something was missing. There was something he had overlooked. Then he realized that the only difference between this transference and that of the river crossing, was the absence of his grip upon the Key. He scurried through his pockets in panic to find the Key. He did not want such an oversight to ruin his safeguarded return. He would take hold of it and attempt, as before, to be precipitously placed upon the river bank and not water. He hated the water.

As he continued the concentration within, he searched for the Key. Finally to his delight, he located and felt the cool touch of its metal. It was warm. As he pulled it out of his pocket, he turned his attention to the transference of the Key from his pocket. He proceeded to clutch the Key near to his chest. He smiled and imagined that he was back in his falling through the abyss and not through the Labyrinths. He imagined that he could feel the wind. It was so very real. The disorientation of the shaft was gone, but he kept his eyes shut in fear that by their opening, the process of his transference would be stopped, and he would find himself back in the Labyrinths. He somehow felt that he was really back, and falling into the abyss, but he was afraid. He decided to put the Key closer to his chest. In the process of this movement, he inadvertently created the correct aerodynamic shape to start a twisting rolling of his body through the air. It made him dizzy. He decided to try and adjust his motions, welcoming this as a sign that he might be returning to his own world, in order to soothe the ill feeling caused by the dizziness. He kept his eyes closed and concentrated. He visualized in his mind the scene of his falling. He visualized the scene of his twisting person and through his thoughts began to manipulate the limbs of his transferring body falling through the abyss. He still considered it just a dream and not real. Just as he was attempting to change the configuration that was causing his tumbling, he was startled by a chilling scream from the deepest recesses of his person:

"**J U L I A N !**"

It was a female's voice. Not the one of the Labyrinths, but another. He knew this voice well.

"Lenore?!" was all that Julian had the chance to utter.

The scream had been both so penetrating and startling, that he let go his grip on the Key. It quickly fell from his hand. Reflexively he opened his eyes in an effort to locate and repossess it. The wind hurt his eyes. They began to water. His eyes confirmed that he was back in his own world. It was real and not a dream. He really had made the transference and was spinning through the air. In the changing viewpoints forced upon him by the twisting, he lost sight of the dropped Key. As he tumbled, he caught a glimpse of the river. It was not far below, though his orientation was confused, he assumed, as it was getting larger and closer, that this was 'below'. He was going to fall into the river. He was contorted around again in the air, and this new view instantly revealed much more concerning his 'abysmal' situation. Below and ahead of him was Merm.

"Oh no!" Julian moaned, as he realized he was back in his world, and no longer in the shaft, just a few instants after he had 'leapt' into the abyss from the Tunnel of Light. He was still in the same danger! It was not as he had wanted or expected. In his own mind he had felt that there had been a much larger passage of time since that leap and his journey into the Labyrinths of Light. In reality, only a few brief instants had passed in this his home world! He was bewildered, but there was no time to think about it. He was caught back in the urgency of the reality in the abyss and the dangers that he had hoped he had escaped.

In the fractions of time that followed these realizations, beyond the realm of any notion of his physical reaction, Julian witnessed the final approach of the river. He witnessed Merm's large splashing entry before him, into its dominion. It was followed by a smaller splash about five lengths to one side of Merm's location—the Key! Both were instantly swallowed up by the majesty of this watery serpent in its violent twisting, rolling action. He knew, like Merm, he was helpless to alter the inevitability of his own submersion. He stole a short breath just before his engulfment into the torrid depths of the river.

Julian felt the entry. The whishing sound of the speeding air as he fell was instantly replaced by a crashing noise followed by a silence. He was covered in wetness. His being imploded into another universe of sensation. As the water enveloped him, all his atmospheric dependent organs were cut off from their source by its overpowering membrane. He held his breath, as he gave a moan against the strain of the entry into the river. The current was tugging him in many directions as he went deeper into its depths. It did not take long for him to be slowed from his fall. He was deep within the water. From the pressure against his ears, he assumed he was close to the river bed. His eyes were open, though they were not of much use naked to the water. All he could see were the bubbles from his entry and the powerful mass of dark liquid that surrounded him.

As the energy of his fall was absorbed by the mass of the water, he quickly was slowed to a halt by the viscosity of the liquid. The downward trip was over. He was alive and well. He had survived the fall without harm, but now he was concerned about his ability to swim his way to the surface of the river with the sole breath of air that was still held within him. He had no notion of how deep he was beneath the surface, but he knew that he must act quickly. Immediately he began to struggle against its strength in an effort to escape to the surface. The current was strong, and he was being carried along with it. He was pushed and pulled. The more effort he made, the more the river seemed to hold him. A panic set in, as his body began to scream for another gulp of life sustaining air.

"*Julian. Remember the time before in the river. Be calm. Focus your thought. There is no danger. All will be as before.*"

The voice was from inside. Julian knew its soft tone. It was the voice that had spoken to him before in the river. It was not the same one as in the Labyrinths, but somehow he understood that it was connected and a part of the same source. He became more calm. Out of an instinct he called out in his mind:

"Father? Is that you?"

This time the inner voicing responded in a slow serene tone:

"Part of me is amongst these thoughts, and more. If it helps you to understand, believe in that part. Focus your mind on my words. Listen to their sound. Absorb from them the strength to prevail here. You must not panic. Do not waste your energy."

During these thoughts Julian forgot his breathless panic within the river. He concentrated on communicating with his 'father'.

"The Key is lost." Julian felt sadness as he thought. He was tired and did not feel that he had the strength to deal with the ramifications of its loss and another fight with the *Evil* to acquire the Key, but he also knew that there was no choice. Until the Key was secured his duty was clear.

"No. It is not. It lies on the bed of this mighty river. But you will not find it before the Evil. Return to Aug. The Key will follow. You will all

be joined in Aug. Find the Marks upon the Throne."

"But how? How can I..."

"You will find the way. Look within yourself. The way is there." the Voice interrupted, and as it spoke, started to become distant. It was no longer conversing with Julian, but directing him, "Concentrate. There is a way. Look within."

As the voice slowly distanced, Julian became more aware of his physical situation within the water. An urgency to find his way back to the surface, back to the air prioritized his actions. He did not have the time to continue his communication with his 'father'. There was so much he wanted to know and say; so much that he still did not understand. Just when he managed to connect, there was always something that drew them away.

"Father?" There was a pause and then came a distant reply.

"You know the way. Look within." There was silence within Julian's thought as the voice disappeared.

There was no rational to what had just occurred. Julian turned his mind back to survival. He felt the power of the river as he was tossed in every direction that the current dictated. No matter how hard he tried at swimming the water continued to command. His breath was nearly gone. In his desperation, he recalled his earlier experience within the river. His breath was also lean, and his mind was screaming out for fresh oxygen. Just when he thought he would explode, a voice was present:

"Do not be afraid. Allow the moment to pass. You will not perish." Julian remembered that he did as the voice beckoned. He relaxed and allowed his being to go limp.

"Think of the surface. Think of the bank."

He complied with the voice. He imagined that he was sitting on the bank on the other side of the narrows where the boulders were to allow the crossing. More and more he saw himself there. It was strange. The more he visualized himself actually there, the more comfortable he was in the water. His concern for fresh air was diminishing. This encouraged him to concentrate more till the only reality in his mind was of himself on the other side of the river sitting on shore. It became more and more real. He closed his eyes. More and more he imagined the scene. Soon he did not even hear the muffled sound of the water all around him, or even its feel. He concentrated further. He actually began to hear the cool night breeze and feel the air blowing against his wet body. He thought to open his eyes, but was afraid to break the vision, his only hope of relief!

He remembered how finally he could not with-stand the temptation to see where he had been pulled by the river. He opened his eyes and dis-covered that he was sitting on the bank on the other side of the river!

"*Stop. Allow me to pass.*" Julian knew what to say. For some reason he brought these words to his consciousness. He pushed them out from him toward the river.

"*Stop. I am the Keeper. The Stoneman's son. Allow me to pass.*"

He decided to take this action. The recalling of his previous experience in the river had some-how sparked the idea. As he spoke the words, he stopped his struggling with the water. He stopped his attempts at swimming. He was limp in the river, waiting for a response.

"*Stop.*"

Julian focused his thought inward just as he had done before when he was submerged. Again he turned his awareness away from his lack of breath and onto the surface out of the water. He visualized that he was floating upward and very near to the membrane separating this watery

world and the world of life sustaining air. He
trusted that he would be alright. He accepted the
reality he was manufacturing in his thought and
disassociated himself with his actual corporeal
condition.

"Stop. Allow me to pass."

He repeated this over and over in his mind, as
he visualized more and more his return to the
surface and his rescue from the watery depths.

Just as in his other river crossing experience,
there was, at first, an imperceptible reaction to his
words and actions. It grew more pronounced and
noticeable the more detached he became from
the reality of his submersion. He could not be
certain as to the reality of his tangible existence.
If he attempted to acknowledge his situation he
would be drawn back to all the uncomfortable-
ness and actuality of that awareness. It would
draw his whole being there. He knew that this
would cause him to perish. He could not allow
himself to be distracted by these thoughts. His
survival depended upon the matter of the pureness of his trust; a faith, an absolute knowing,
without the slightest speck of doubt or distraction. He must be completely, willingly accepting
of his security. This acceptance was not of the
nature of wishful thinking. It was more a leap of

unadulterated faith. There was no need for him
to be concerned with *that* awareness, as it was not
able to affect him as long as he undeniably
trusted in himself and the direction that he had
chosen to travel toward. It was an inward journey. A trip that would deliver him as fast as his
commitment to it was made. The slightest doubt
or reticence would prevent his secure deliver-
ance. The longer he allowed himself to be
trapped to the reality of the river and its response
or reaction to his words, the longer he would be
agonized by that reality. He had, therefore, no
confirmation of the changes that were occurring—nor did he need any! He trusted in his inward choice. He knew he was following the direction that would return him to his proper
world. He did not dare to check or reassure himself of the situation. There was no need. He
trusted. He knew. The River was reacting faster
as Julian's 'trust' began to dominate his being.
The water slowly sensed the Magic of the
Balance within him. It heard the faint words
within him as he was tossed by its current.

The Pass River was an old source of water
originating deep within the canyons of Tika. It,
like the luminescent plants, had acquired a certain amount of the Magic of the Old Ones of

Tika during their long inhabitancy there in side
its solid stone canyons. As the Old Ones had developed in their discoveries and knowing of the
Magic of the Balance, they had imparted a residual energy of the Magic through osmosis, to the
river. They had been great travelers as they
searched their Worlds for the meaning and ways
of invincibility, using the River as it was first
called, to pass from world to world in their
search. Initially, this mighty River had been
harsh and unforgiving to their passage, much
like a wild untamed beast trying to throw an un-
invited Rider. It had risen up against any who
entered or attempted to transverse its watery epi-
dermis. This made travel arduous and dangerous. Alternate routes from the River were made,
but there were many other dangers along these
routes which impeded their journeys. It became
paramount to find a solution, so that their travels
could be conducted with a minimal amount of
concern.

The Old Ones soon managed, with their increasing knowledge and Magic of the Balance, to
tame the River. They managed to adjust it to
calm and allow passage to all of their kind. Once
this process of taming was complete, it became
known as the Pass River.

The River would, upon request, allow passage once it sensed the Magic of the Old Ones within the requesting traveler. It would calm and allow them to safely travel. As time and use had increased, the verbal request of the Old Ones was replaced by the mutual sensing of the Pass River and traveler. An intimate connection and affinity developed; a linking through the Magic of the Balance. This was the way of invincibility. The collective well-being and harmony of everything. A cooperativeness that enhanced all; a trusting of the workings of the Balance by the users of the Magic.

To gain this manipulation, the River was approached through the Balance within the Magic. There was a connecting made. The Old Ones caused the River to lower its natural barriers and expose its elements within the Balance. There were certain aspects of its fundamental elements that could then be attuned. It was through the Old Ones knowledge within the great Magic and the ways of invincibility, that these elements could be altered. It was a process that bonded both parties eternally through the Balance. There was a mutual giving and receiving, a trusting in the pureness of the understanding of the simplicity of a meaning of existence that reestablished the harmony within the Balance. Trusting was a required factor to initiate the process of invincibility.

To all others, the River remained brutal and wild, just as it had been for the Old Ones before their knowledge and understanding of the existence of the Balance and its Magic was discovered, developed, and prudently exploited. The River was a natural barrier to keep the unprepared, unknowing, unwelcome traveler from entering the zone of Tika and learning of the power of the Magic and the Balance before they were ready to hold such knowledge. In the wrong minds a great unraveling could occur.

Until the initial discoveries by the Old Ones, there had not been much natural concern over these matters. After the uncovering of the Magic by the Old Ones, a passage had been opened that any could follow thereafter. Resultantly, the River's waters continued to deter those not of the Old Ones that might wish to pass. It would rise up from a calm and turn back those others who attempted to go along it.

The dangers and corruption of the power of the Magic though intricate, were realized and dealt with by the Old Ones. Dorluc had been the first sign of the potential hazards of the knowledge of the Magic and lure of the words of invincibility to those who lusted for power. Their self interest would abuse and misuse the Magic and ultimately end in their own, as well as the worlds, unraveling. A process that once begun could not be reversed. The Old Ones wisdom realized and foresaw the potentialities of their discoveries. They understood the true meaning, use and intricacy of invincibility. The *Passwords* needed to be protected, the Balance retained, and the lust of such *Evil* kept at bay.

Farther down its course it was less threatening, but in the North and closer to Tika it was vehement in dissuading the traveler from pursuing any farther. The only exceptions made were to those of the Magic of the Balance; those who possessed the knowledge or Magic of the Old Ones.

Once the Old Ones had uncovered the meaning and ways of invincibility, and that knowledge became more centralized within the zone, Tika became a sacred place for the Chosen who lived there. The Old Ones established a second more public home in the City that Sparkled or what was later to become Norkleau. The 'City' became a center attracting all sorts, while Tika became more and more remote and inaccessible to all but the Old Ones. It became an underground city, secluded and mysterious. As a remembrance, a small temple structure was built in plain view on the highest canyon top. It was said to be a sacred place of philosophy and thought; a place of exclusion from the outside worlds. Outsiders were not welcomed. Out of a respect and a fear, Tika was ignored, whilst the 'City' grew and prospered.

The real Tika lay far beneath the canyon top temple. It was an underground community, with a myriad of connecting passageways, chambers and levels. It was here that the Old Ones continued their enlightenment and at the same time conservation and protection of the Balance. They secretly continued their travels throughout the worlds. They appeared and disappeared without trace. This was accomplished by the vast network of passageways that were hidden from all others, and their safe use of the Pass River. They understood not to intervene with the development of the other worlds, but did try to guide them away from poorer choices and the dangers that might exist when discovered. This assistance was given without the worlds awareness. The Old Ones developed a network of moles within certain individuals through out the worlds. Through these moles, suggestions could be made to the various worlds.

The Old Ones never were seen by these worlds. Only the myths of their temple were known. The myths were revered and feared, and the mystery of the Old Ones was never revealed. So much peace and harmony had existed for so long, that when the 'City' began to go into a decline, the other worlds were too content and self involved to notice. When finally the Old Ones had quietly gone on, the Worlds were operating so smoothly that no one had known of their passing. It was believed for the longest time that they were still hidden away somewhere in the Worlds.

Gradually the 'City' fell to ruin and the memory of the Old Ones was relegated to the mythology of the origin of the Worlds. All had been in Balance until the influencing of Dorluc and his *Evil*. He had influenced the rising up of the Gotts and the Separation War. The Worlds no longer resided in the safe dominion of the Old Ones. Only the long dormant moles and the Chosen, were left to save the Balance. Only the Chosen could activate the process to protect the worlds. Only the Chosen could access the Magic.

Julian, Darla, Eruinn, and Thiunn were Chosen. Because the threat that caused them to awaken was of such power and duration, they were now in the earliest stages of a permanent change. If they managed to protect the Balance, they would never be the same again. This applied to not only them, but to others of whom they were not yet completely aware. A new order was being created. Now that the *Evil* had initiated the process to discover the *Passwords*, the Worlds would require the existence of the Chosen to watch over and guide them all away from the wrong choices, just as the Old Ones had done. Not only were Julian, Darla, Eruinn and Thiunn awakening to protect the Balance, they were also now going through a rite of passage. A rite that if survived, would transform them to things that even they did not fully comprehend. Their awakenings had begun to accumulate and now their residual knowing had grown to the point where it was too large to be forgotten. They must learn, and in time they would.

The river was strong. All around were little white caps of trapped air being pulled and torn through the water. Julian opened his eyes as he allowed his body to be tossed.

"Stop. Allow me to pass." he directed his thought again outward. This time he noticed that the water was less violent in his immediate vicin-

ity. The water was slowing. Its current was getting calmer. He was no longer being thrown back a forth by the current. He noted that there was a funnel forming within the water. A funnel that he was in the middle of. It was not the same type of shaft as the Labyrinths. It was a narrow funnel of water amidst the river that was calm. All of the water of the river around it was forcing itself by, but this shaft was calm and unaffected. Julian turned his head up towards the surface of the river. The funnel rose all the way up. Without further question or amazement, he pushed his arms above his head and kicked his legs. He moved upward through the still funnel as he pulled his arms down. He swam with more confidence as he understood the meaning of the funnel. The River was allowing him to pass. It had heard the ancient command and after identifying the source had responded in the required fashion. This one would pass unharmed.

The distance to the surface seemed to take forever to cross. Julian's air was expired, but he felt no discomfort. He continued in the effort to get to the surface. One, two, three, four, five, six, seven, stroke after stroke was made. As he came closer to the surface he noted that the water in the funnel was of a different color than the rest

of the surrounding river water. It wasn't just the
light from the surface changing the hue. There
seemed to be a yellow green tint to the channel.
It reminded Julian of the luminescent plants that
he had encountered in the underground passageways. He did not spend long on this thought,
but merely noted the difference. By the time he
had taken twelve strokes, he knew he was almost
returned. He could feel the pressure of the water
diminishing as he approached the surface. He
understood what this meant. He was very close to
the membrane at the surface. As he looked
ahead he was able to see the film that separated
this liquid world from the atmosphere of his
world. It was a floating blurred spot. He pulled
two more times, then felt as his hands pierced
through the membrane and into the dry air. In
moments his head and torso were also through,
and he was gasping for air.

It felt good. The water was dripping over his
face as he swept it away from his mouth and
nose with his right hand. He then blinked several
times and rubbed away the moisture from his
eyes so that he could focus his sight. He was in
the middle of the river. Towering above him on
both sides were the tremendous canyons. It was
dusk. He was not sure how far he had traveled

along in the river, or even how long he had been submerged. He assumed it could not have been very long. He paddled himself around in a circle to try and get his bearings, as he maintained his body half in and out of the water. Directly behind him about four hundred lengths was a huge rock that separated the river into two channels. The canyon walls were at either side, and ahead the run of the river. He was being held in place within the river by the funnel. Julian considered his next challenge. He must get to shore.

As he considered his circumstances his eye caught an area of the canyon near the bank that seemed to be a path. It was on the far bank. He thought that would be a good spot to cross to and then get out of the river. From there Julian believed he would be able to find a way beyond the entrapment of the steep canyons and river.

Instantly the funnel that was holding him in position in the water began to move him through the river to that spot. He no longer was treading water, but was being propelled toward that spot on the bank. He felt no motion through the water. It was as if he were traveling through the air. There was no pressure on his body, nor any wake from his passage. The journey was seamless.

In moments he was in the shallows at the bank. His feet touched the rock bottom and he literally walked out of the river. With a little effort he walked to the path which was a length up from the slope of the bank. He turned to see if the funnel was still in the river and suddenly became aware of the river's noise. The roar was deafening and oddly soothing. Shivers went up his spine and his skin tightened. It was a pleasant caress. As this occurred, he watched as the area where the funnel had been was quickly engulfed by the fury of the river. The funnel had dissipated within moments of his safe landing upon the path on the bank. The river seemed to be able to sense his well-being. Julian marveled at the feat. He drew in a long breath of the clean fresh moist river air. He was happy to have survived.

Survived? Julian's mind was jarred into the realization that the Lord Merm might also have survived. Especially, since he now realized how much the *Evil* was helping the Gott Lord. Julian recalled more of the Magical events that had happened over this journey from Jard. He wondered why he had not recalled this before. Merm was nearby. He was being watched, like he had been in the Burning Forest. A sense of the urgency of his quest was re-established. He must hurry.

Julian stretched his head back and looked way up the canyon walls. He was thinking of the Tunnel of Light and the events that had led him to jump from the opening into the abyss. He searched but was not able to find the opening. He was not sure where it was. In his thoughts beyond the din of the river he was speaking to himself:

"I must find my way back to them."

He needed to find Darla, Eruinn and Thiunn. He sensed their presence; especially Darla. He could sense her smooth skin and smell. He took in a deep breath through his nose as he recalled. He missed her more than his nephews. He longed to be with her again, and he knew he would. They were still here. He was not worried for their safety. He knew that the fight in the Cavern of Three had not scathed them. He also knew that they were no longer in the Cavern; that they were nearby. From within he knew that he must find them. They would help. He did not yet know how, but he knew he needed them with him now. He paused in these thoughts and began to drift within the Magic. His connection was now stronger within the Balance. She was near.

They were near. He knew their presence. They were not far away. He would be with them in moments.

About the Author

Terence Munsey lives in Toronto, Ontario. He attended York University for undergraduate studies and then Stanford University for graduate studies, where he received an M.A. degree.

He has written four books in *The Stoneman Series:*

1. THE FLIGHT OF THE STONEMAN'S SON
2. THE KEEPER OF THREE
3. LABYRINTHS OF LIGHT
4. MARKS OF STONE

He loves to hear from his readers. Send or fax him a letter.

*Send $2.00 today and get your *official* 2&1/4in **STONEMAN SERIES** button.